THE *Future* KING

kiru taye

Kiru Taye

First Published in Great Britain in 2022 by
LOVE AFRICA PRESS
103 Reaver House, 12 East Street, Epsom KT17 1HX
www.loveafricapress.com

Text copyright © Kiru Taye, 2022

ISBN: 978-1-914226-25-0
Also available in ebook format

ROYAL HOUSE OF SAENE

THE PRINCESSES:
His Defiant Princess by Nana Prah

His Inherited Princess by Empi Baryeh

His Captive Princess by Kiru Taye

THE PRINCES:
The Torn Prince by Zee Monodee

The Resolute Prince by Nana Prah

The Tainted Prince by Kiru Taye

The Illegitimate Prince by Empi Baryeh

The Future King by Kiru Taye

BLURB

Prince Azikiwe didn't get the 'Player Zik' moniker by chance. Life is for living, and rules are boring. Then his older brother jilts his betrothed and abdicates his royal title. Suddenly, the constrictive Crown Prince title is thrust upon Zik, and his partying days come to an abrupt halt. The least of his worries, though. Now, he contends with the scorned, furious bride chosen for him and a nation at risk of falling into anarchy. Does he have what it takes to become the future king?

PLAYLIST

Flowers ~ Arrdee
Where Do Broken Hearts Go ~ Whitney Houston
Giving You The Best That I've Got ~ Anita Baker
Have You Ever Really Loved A Woman ~ Bryan Adams
You Got It ~ Roy Orbison
Levels ~ Flavour

CHAPTER ONE

July 2020, Bagumi
"Some people use funerals to chase skirts undercover!"

Prince Azikiwe dan Ibrahim Saene read the tweet and winced, averting his gaze. The sprawling green landscape and silvery waters of the Lake Miri estates came into view as the helicopter approached, the whirring rotors a muted background sound with the noise-reduction headphones.

A few seconds later, his gaze returned to his smartphone, and a reluctant smile curled the corner of his lips as he reread the caustic post Princess Amara Onoh had shared yesterday after a picture of Zik and a female friend had appeared on social media.

Of course, he had known @theonohprincess had been referring to him as soon as he'd seen the caption. The woman had been taking swipes at him and riding his ass for a few years and not in a pleasurable way, like a tick burrowed under his skin he couldn't eradicate.

Caustic or not, he was compelled to read her online opinions. Compelled to engage in their ridiculous battles and respond accordingly. Still, his comeback of *"Some people should have empathy for those in mourning!"* on this occasion had been less than lacklustre.

Running his personal account, @playerzik, he was usually savvy and sometimes savage when it came to virtual banter. Yet, when it came to Amara, he found himself tongue-tied and restrained.

For one, she was his best friends' baby sister. Secondly, she was his sister Isha's best friend. Lastly and most crucially, she was his older brother Zawadi's fiancée and would be Zik's full-fledged sister-in-law and a member of the Saene royal family in a few months.

Therefore, although Amara baited him frequently like it was a part-time hobby, his hands were tied, and he could never respond with the full severity some of her comments deserved.

In any case, why did she always snipe at him when he appeared in photos with other women? She was engaged to his brother. So, what was her problem?

What ticked her off? Why did she automatically assume he had sex with every woman he met? That would be irresponsible and grossly inappropriate in a lot of cases.

Over the years, he'd acquired a reputation as a playboy and had been linked with different famous ladies—international movie stars, musicians, models, and socialites. However, it didn't mean he lacked scruples. His lovers were always unattached, consenting adults who knew the score right from the start and wanted to scratch a very temporary itch. Full stop.

Why did Amara love to insinuate something sinister lurked behind his every move?

The gentle jolt of the copter landing on the green lawn roused him from his reverie. He tucked his phone into his pocket, shaking his head to dispel thoughts of Amara. He had other, more pressing matters to focus on. Like the summons to visit his father today.

In the distance loomed the manor located in a designated area of outstanding natural beauty, one of the royal residences of His Majesty King Ibrahim dan Aziz Saene of the Kingdom of Bagumi.

Unlike Darusa Palace—or DP as it was fondly known—located in the bustling metropolis, Lake Miri was a country house in the middle of a reserve, surrounded by farmlands and plantations. While DP became his official home from his teenage years onward, Lake Miri held some of Zik's earliest memories. His ancestors had been born here, including his father, which made it very significant to his family.

So being called here, to discuss a delicate family matter, no less, must mean something significant. What, though?

Last night's phone conversation with his brother replayed in his mind.

"Papa wants to see you at Lake Miri tomorrow. Six p.m.," Zawadi said after the initial pleasantries.

"Sure. What's it about?" Zik replied, trying to gauge if this would be an informal family gathering or a formal royal conference. The senior active members of the royal family met once every quarter to discuss duties. Zik attended when required. Otherwise, he avoided these meetings.

"Something's come up. Sorry about the short notice, but it's an urgent matter." His brother sounded ominous.

Unease wormed through Zik's gut. They'd been cautious, but the pandemic had dealt a few surprising blows already. "Everyone is alive and well, right?"

He hoped his brother would tell him if it was bad news rather than keep him in suspense for twenty-four hours, which would be cruel.

"Of course. Everyone is well. It's nothing of the sort. Just a matter of state," Zawadi reassured.

"Oh. Good. See you tomorrow then." Relieved, he exhaled.

Had he been wrong to exhale in relief back then? Being here brought on a different vibe, one that hung like an ominous dark cloud over him.

Zik disembarked the helicopter, ducked under the whirring blades, and walked down the long, stately drive towards the impressive mansion, his personal bodyguard two paces to his right. Palace employees in buggies trundled past, carrying the luggage. He could've opted to be transferred by a royal buggy from the helipad to the front door, but he'd rather stretch his legs after hours confined in aircrafts. Plus, the fresh air would do him good, and clear the shroud of darkness threatening to encroach on him.

He'd flown in from Abuja, Nigeria to Darusa, Bagumi by private jet before hopping on the helicopter for the transfer to Lake Miri.

A close friend and member of the Bagumian Princes' Rugby team had passed away recently following a short illness, and Zik had been in Nigeria over the weekend for the funeral.

The full princes' squad should have been there. However, the global viral pandemic meant there had been restrictions on number of attendees at the burial ceremony, thus necessitating Zik's presence as squad representative. Also present had been his best friends and teammates, Ekene and Ejike Onoh, who lived in Nigeria and hadn't needed to acquire special travel documents.

A sigh escaped Zik. Bagumi had been in full lockdown for three months, from April to July, and although it was a small country, they'd controlled the number of COVID-19 cases to a soft peak, which meant they'd opened quicker than most. Their scientists worked tirelessly on early detection methods, tracking and tracing possible cases, and developing vaccines with the worldwide scientific collective in an unprecedented effort.

This had been Zik's first trip outside Bagumi in months. After Isha's wedding, he'd added her International Trade portfolio to his Natural Resources cabinet duties, which meant he travelled often. However, the last three months had seen his longest stint in his country without duty—or pleasure—related visits abroad.

It hurt him that the opportunity had arisen from such a dire event as a death. He'd grieved, mourned, paid his respects.

However, the trip had brought a ray of light bursting through the gloom. The chance to spend time with his besties, two-thirds of the Onoh princes. Earlier today, they'd been at a hotel with outdoor facilities, watching the Hungarian F1 Grand Prix on a big screen under an awning. A huge car-racing enthusiast, in any other year, he probably would have been present in Hungary for this event.

Although they'd watched the exciting race, the mood had been sombre, each person sipping their drink quietly. Yet, being with his friends wasn't always about the conversations. It had more to do with the company. Before the pandemic, they'd spent almost every other weekend together at some event or just hanging out. Ejike and Ekene understood him and being in the same physical space boosted his energy.

Zik would readily admit the pandemic quarantine period had been almost hellish for him. He didn't do well in isolation. He was a people person and needed to communicate with others, to see and touch them where possible because he was naturally tactile with the people he loved. However, these days, he had to restrain himself, making it immensely frustrating sometimes.

Of course, his family was there, but due to their quarantine buddy system, he was kind of isolated.

For the lockdown, his parents had gone to Lake Miri. His sisters were married and lived in different countries. Zediah sheltered in place with his young family in DP. Zareb went with his fiancée, Malika, to their home in Darusa. Zawadi was in Somie with Danai, his principal protection officer. Although Zik would swear his brother was in love with the covert agent slash bodyguard—there'd been *something* there...

Nevertheless, the arrangement had left him alone and he'd retreated to his Onyi stronghold of Beya, at his wits' end stalking the Beya Castle corridors like a ghost. He'd ended up volunteering at the local pandemic relief centre, distributing palliative packages to the community just so he could have interactions with other humans beyond video conferences. He'd even been hands on with the donation of digital devices to the local secondary students so they could carry on with their home learning when the schools barred physical attendance.

Now, he strode towards his parent's country residence, the uneasy feeling from last night returning to churn heavy acid in his stomach. What was so important and urgent to require this gathering when they'd avoided physical meetings for months because the king had a heart condition?

"Welcome to Lake Miri Palace, Your Highness." The butler bowed, along with the other staff all wearing partial face coverings.

"Thank you." Keeping his black mask on, Zik sauntered into the expansive foyer with stone flooring, high ceiling, and a grand staircase. Although he'd been tested and cleared before the flight from Nigeria, he wouldn't take any chances.

On the dark-wood table in the corner stood a gilded white vase of fresh flowers and a golden-white bottle of aloe vera antibacterial hand gel. He pumped a couple of squirts into his palm and massaged his hands.

"There you are." His mother entered the lobby in a flurry of blue butterfly lace boubou, her hair wrapped in a matching stylish turban, feet in silver diamante slippers.

A smile spread across his face as he bowed. "The queen of my heart."

"I've told you that title should be reserved for the love of your life." She slid her arm through his elbow instead of hugging him like she did before the pandemic, considering they were both tactile. Still, she pulled him into her side for a few seconds, and he went willingly.

"And right now, you are the love of my life." He grinned as they strolled through the corridor, shoes thudding on the hard flooring. No matter his previous mood, seeing his birth mother gave him joy.

"You are incorrigible." Her laughter resonated like a gentle, warm tinkle. "So how was your trip? How are the Onohs?"

Some of Zik's previous unease returned. "Honestly, the trip was depressing. I thought watching the Grand Prix and LH winning would cheer me up. But it didn't last long."

"That's to be expected, love. You buried one of your closest friends on Friday. He was gone too soon. You should allow yourself time to grieve."

His mother was correct. But life didn't stop because of loss and grief. There were obligations to fulfil, like this meeting. Then again, seeing his parents wasn't really an obligation...except when they started hounding him to settle down.

His siblings had already paired up with their life partners. Except Zawadi whose wedding was scheduled for September.

Hang on. Was that the reason for this gathering? The pandemic had messed up many plans, resulting in some wedding cancellations. Perhaps...

"Mum, what's the purpose of the meeting?" he asked, trying not to jump ahead of himself. No point imagining unlikely scenarios. His mother was a well of information when it came to family matters and always happy to fill him in.

"Why? Aren't you happy to see me?" She gave him a side glance. Her brown eyes twinkled with amusement, taking the harshness from her words.

He chuckled and squeezed her hand. "Of course, I'm always pleased to see you, queen of my heart. I just want to find out what you know."

"You'll find out soon enough when Zawadi arrives."

He did a pretend surprise jerk and spoke in a teasing, conspiratorial tone. "Is it supposed to be a secret? You have to tell me now."

His mother giggled. "It's not supposed to be a secret, silly boy. Didn't you know Zawadi went to see Danai's parents a few days ago about marrying her? He's coming to formally present her to your father."

"Oh." Zik's insides went cold. So, *something* had definitely been going on there. "Zawadi is going to marry Amara *and* Danai?"

His mother's dainty shoulders lifted and fell. "We'll find out when he gets here."

Shit. Months ago, he'd had an argument with his oldest brother about Danai, a covert agent sent by the Bagumi Intelligence Service to investigate the palace mole involved in a failed assassination attempt on Zawadi's life. She'd acted as Zawadi's principal protection officer until the spy had been caught weeks ago.

Zik had confronted his brother because Zawadi had sacked Danai from their rugby squad unfairly, and it had become apparent that his older brother had feelings for her. But Zawadi had denied it and supposedly cut off any personal interactions with Danai. Zik had made an offhand comment at the time about Zawadi marrying two wives like their father.

Then Covid happened, and Danai became Zawadi's quarantine buddy, moving to the Somie country house with him for lockdown.

Now, Zawadi was coming to present Danai as his fiancée?

Was his brother really going to wed two women?

Zik's stomach rolled with dread. He'd thought burying a friend would be the lowest point of the weekend. But he had the sinking feeling it was about to get a lot worse.

CHAPTER TWO

"My son. Do you understand the consequence of that statement?"

The king spoke quietly. Dressed in a multi-layered blue and black robe, head covered in a turban, he sat on an upholstered armchair carved from special iroko-wood and embedded with gemstones.

The consorts sat on gilded, padded armchairs on either side of him—to the right Queen Zulekha, the first wife, and Zawadi's mother. On the left, Queen Sapphire, second wife and Zik's mother.

Zawadi had just presented Danai as his chosen life partner to their parents, which had been expected. However, he'd also confirmed he would not marry his current fiancée, which had drawn shocked expressions from their parents, prompting the question from their father.

"Yes, Papa," Zawadi replied. He stood in the middle of the reception room, facing their parents. He wore a similar ceremonial flowing tunic and trouser set like their father, this time in purple, making Zik the odd one out in his European two-piece navy suit, white shirt, and red tie.

"I understand that by not marrying Amara Onoh," his brother continued, "I'm giving up my rights to the throne. It was not an easy decision for me to make. All my life, I have been prepared for the crown. I've spent the time doing what everyone expected me to do but not what I wanted to do. Until Danai came along. For the first time in my life, I feel like I'm finally living on my own terms."

"You can still have it all," Queen Zulekha interjected. "Just keep to the marriage contract with Amara Onoh. As I said, I'll make her understand. You can marry both. Or does your new *love* not understand our traditions?"

Danai's jawline tightened visibly. She stood beside Zawadi, looking already like a princess in a maxi teal tulle dress and black leather heels, a teal scarf loosely covering her chignon.

Zik ached with sympathy for the woman. He liked her. Although she was a commoner, she didn't deserve Zawadi's mother's contempt. Queen Zulekha did not tolerate women with zero blue blood as royal consorts, as evidenced by her still-ongoing rejection of Riona, Zediah's wife, even after more than a year of marriage. Malika had escaped her wrath because the queen had engineered that pairing. Danai would have her work cut out for her.

"Your Majesty, I understand tradition. I love your son and will stand by his decisions. However, I will not share his bed with another woman," Danai spoke up, and rightly so.

Bravo! Zik cheered her silently.

"I agree with Danai," Zawadi said. "We are content with each other. She is the only woman for me. I pray for your blessing, Papa."

His father sighed and nodded. "You have it, my son. I wish you and your chosen the joys of a happy union."

With those words, King Ibrahim Saene dissolved Zawadi's betrothal to Amara Onoh and gave his consent for Zawadi to marry Danai an hour after Zik arrived at Lake Miri.

The statement echoed in Zik's head as he stared at his brother, trying to pinpoint his emotions—a potent mixture of fury and shock.

Shock because their father had just annulled Zawadi's ten-year betrothal to Amara. Fury because the king had acted like this was no big deal.

The gasps and incredulous expressions on the queens' faces spoke volumes. A lot of money, sweat, and tears had gone into securing that marriage contract. It had been all for nothing. Dissolved with one pronouncement. No consequences whatsoever for Zawadi.

His brother had just screwed up a massive deal for their family, and their father hadn't even blinked. He'd waved it off as if it was of no importance.

Fury won and coursed through Zik's veins as he curled his hands into fists, his jaw tense.

Zawadi was jilting Amara, a woman he'd been betrothed to for over a decade. Not to mention the diplomatic incident bound to arise. How was no one concerned about diplomacy at such a time? Especially after everything Bagumi had already been through, starting with the shitstorm that had erupted when Zediah and Bilkiss Noda had refused to marry?

Amara's family were close to the Saenes. Zik had known them for as long as he could remember. The Onoh siblings and the Saene siblings had grown up together. They'd spent time in each other's family homes regularly.

He'd watched Amara grow from a rather bratty child into the regal woman whose name was whispered reverently among men.

Zik would admit to being one of those men, once upon a time. But his fantasies had been snuffed out before they could take wings and fly. He'd accepted Zawadi would marry Amara one day.

Now as the day drew near, Zawadi had turned her down. Just like that.

Hell.

Zik closed his eyes and took deep inhales and slow exhales while everyone else in the reception room congratulated the new couple. Joy seemed to be the order of the day. But he needed to contain his anger in the presence of his parents. In any case, he was supposed to be the easy-going one, the fun one, the charming one.

On any other day, he would be giving his brother a bear hug and planning the celebrations, especially the stag do. Any excuse for a party— music, people, and hedonistic pleasures.

Therefore, he should plaster a smile on his face and wish his brother well for getting engaged *again*! Just like everyone else was doing. But the churning acid had morphed into a fire boulder which now seemed wedged somewhere between his trachea and his abdomen, almost choking him.

He couldn't even explain the twisted emotions engulfing him. Mostly because he couldn't figure out what had just happened, not on a deep level.

He should be happy because his brother had found love and wouldn't marry Amara. Yet, Zik couldn't seem to muster any cheer as he watched Zawadi prostrate again and touch their father's velvet-slippered feet.

"Thank you, Papa," the Crown Prince professed.

"Congratulations, both of you," Zik finally managed, but his voice sounded croaky and not as cheerful as it should be. Thankfully, he didn't have to attempt an embrace with Zawadi due to social-distancing rules.

"Thanks, Zik." His brother straightened and returned to Danai's side.

"Thank you, Prince Azikiwe."

The woman's tentative smile reached the part of Zik disposed to making everyone comfortable.

Sure, the past few months had been stressful, and he was having a bad weekend—first, a friend's funeral, then the Twitter spat with Amara, and now this. But he'd had bad days before. He could compartmentalise his feelings and unpack them later.

Moreover, Danai was his friend. At least, he hoped they were friends, and she was going to become his sister-in-law. Standing there in coordinated outfits with Zawadi, they looked every bit like a royal couple.

So, he relaxed his facial muscles and allowed thoughts of happier times to return to his mind, offering a natural grin. "No need to be so formal since we're now family. Just call me Zik like everyone else does."

"Thank you," she said, settling in an armchair opposite him as Zawadi sat in another close to her.

Zik narrowed his eyes at them. The way Zawadi gazed at his fiancée and maintained physical proximity without touching her indicated the depths of his feelings for her. His brother was obviously smitten with Danai.

And Danai was good people. He had gotten to know her well when she'd joined their rugby squad. He had no doubt she was good for his brother, the evidence there to see in their interactions.

Still, Zawadi's statement from earlier this evening came back to haunt him.

"I understand that by not marrying Amara Onoh, I'm giving up my rights to the throne."

Zik was next-in-line to the throne after Zawadi. If his older brother gave up his rights to the crown, then Zik was *it*.

Fuck.

A chill travelled down his spine, alerting him, and he forced out the dreaded question no one else seemed ready to confront. "What does this mean with regards to the succession?"

He needed clarifications. Although he was technically next-in-line, he had other brothers, and his father wielded the power to name whomever he chose as Crown Prince. The king had once jokingly implied he would've named Isha as the heir if she'd been male. Therefore, Zik wouldn't hold out hope of being named. Zareb, his youngest brother, was disciplined and would make a better king, probably.

"It means—" his father's voice cut through his reverie. "—that we must make arrangements for the next in line to become Crown Prince, and that is you, Azikiwe. I—"

"Hang on a minute," Queen Zulekha interrupted, shaking her head, eyes narrowed. "You can't really be thinking about taking the succession away from Zawadi. He is still Crown Prince."

She had a good point. Zawadi hadn't changed as a person because he had chosen a different wife. He was still a capable and dutiful man who would govern the country like he'd been raised to do regardless of his spouse.

However, many years ago, their parents had made a marriage pact with Amara's parents— Amara would marry the Saene Crown Prince—that had been enshrined in the Bagumian constitution. No other way around it.

The origins of the family relationship went back to the Biafran war in the late 1960s when Amara's father had been a child and his parents had sent him into exile to Bagumi. The Saene royal family had sheltered him, and the country had offered refuge to thousands of Igbo refugees. Many of the children who came to Bagumi during that time never returned to Nigeria for various reasons, mostly because their known relatives had been killed during the genocide. Those who'd stayed grew up and set up homes and businesses in Bagumi. This Igbo community became a large part of what made

Bagumi successful because they brought their entrepreneurial talents and thrived in commerce as well as technology.

Amara's wedding to Zawadi was supposed to solidify the ties between Bagumi and Igboland. The entire country had been looking forward to it. So, a broken engagement meant terrible news for Bagumi. Not to mention how it would damage the Saene relationship with the Onohs.

"But you just heard him." His father waved a hand towards Zawadi. "He made that position untenable for himself when he chose a different wife. Azikiwe is next-in-line and is available to marry the Onoh princess. You don't have any objections to marrying her, do you, son?"

The king directed his dark gaze at Zik, along with everyone else in the room.

Talk of being put on the spot! Zik pressed his lips together in a slight grimace, and his gaze ping-ponged around the room.

His first response was no. He didn't want to marry the Onoh princess. She was Zawadi's fiancée. Had been his brother's betrothed for over thirteen years until a few minutes ago. Zik had programmed his mind to categorize her in the most innocuous ways possible.

Zawadi's fiancée.

Ejike's and Ekene's kid sister.

Isha's best friend.

A.K.A. the only safe labels to use for her because anything else was just...

No, he wasn't going back there. Wasn't going to resurrect the teenage boy who'd wanted something different.

Simply put, Amara was out of bounds. Nothing more.

Now everyone else was looking at him expectantly. He felt their stares prickling his skin.

"Papa, is there no other option?" he asked before he could think better of it.

"Azikiwe!"

His mother's tone chided, her expression pensive. He could imagine her concern because he wasn't taking the opportunity to be crown prince eagerly. But she knew his heart more than anyone else in this room and would support his decisions. She had never let him down.

"Son, do you have an objection to marrying her?" His father sounded frustrated.

Of course, he would be displeased by Zik's reticent. Papa generally ignored him except for the moments when he required Zik to perform duties Zawadi couldn't or wouldn't do. Zik had never lived up to his father's expectations while the old man could see no wrong in Zawadi.

To them, Zawadi was a paradigm of virtue while Zik was an epitome of vice.

His brother had always been their father's favourite and closest child. Evidence shown in how his brother had just dissolved a decades-long agreement which could cause political problems for their country.

Yet, their father hadn't frowned at him with the same disappointed expression he focused on Zik now because Zik wasn't living up to the dutiful Zawadi standard and accepting his new fate as next-in-line.

Zik would laugh if the situation wasn't so grave. Nobody expected his resistance, it seemed. And he couldn't blame them.

He was the people-pleaser around here. The fixer. The one who went out of his way to make sure everyone else was comfortable. The price he paid for them to leave him to his *vices*, his parties, his lifestyle.

But now, they would take it all away. By binding him to a marriage he didn't choose and a country he didn't want to rule.

And they didn't think he'd have a few objections?

For goodness' sake, they were offering him as a substitute to Amara. She was Zawadi's ex. His brother's forsaken. A harsh reality.

Moreover, had anyone even considered the princess's opinion? Why would she want Zik as husband?

"Papa, I'm just wondering ... What if she doesn't want to marry me? She wanted Zawadi. And I'm not him."

He and Zawadi were as different as fire and ice. On the face of it, the only similarity came from their bloodline—half of it, at least. For as long as Zik could remember, Zawadi had wanted to be king while he had been the opposite.

Now, he wanted to ask his brother what kind of mad love had struck him to make him think of giving up his birth right, something he'd wanted to do all his life.

His father sighed. "I understand, son. But we'll cross that bridge when we get to it. For now, I need to know that you're willing to go through with the marriage. We can't afford to let them down."

And this was the crux of it. Zik couldn't let his family down. If Zawadi was stepping aside, then all the heavy responsibilities would pass onto the next-in-line.

Party animal or not, he was still a dutiful prince. The one who cleaned up the messes. Just another day, just another problem to fix.

What else could he do, really? He puffed out a resigned breath.

"I accept to marry Amara," he said solemnly, the heavy weight of the words settling on his shoulders like a ton of bricks.

"Then it's settled—"

"No, it's not!" Zawadi's mother interrupted the king yet again. "Azikiwe is unsuitable to be Crown Prince. You can't possibly let him become the future king."

The words slammed into Zik like a physical punch, and he jerked in his seat. The words shot out before he could process them in his head. "Why not, Mama? Why am I unsuitable?"

He had never wanted the throne of Bagumi. Had always been content to be the second son, a spare, just like his younger brothers. He'd never thought a day like this would arise when his suitability to be the king would be discussed by his parents. Yet, now, he was considered unsuitable.

His lungs constricted, making it difficult to breathe. Did he not have King Ibrahim's blood running in his veins?

Queen Zulekha met his gaze, her expression devoid of emotion. "You know the reason."

He'd known the first consort all his life, considered her to be his second mother. But he'd never seen her look at him like she was doing now. While their father would make the final decision, it was no secret Queen Zulekha had his ear and was his chief strategist when it came to politics. If she thought him unsuitable, then his father could reject him.

But right now, he itched to know what she had to say. Getting an answer at this very gathering proved primordial.

"No, I don't." Zik kept a blank face, staying inscrutable. While he wasn't the most aloof of his siblings, he could maintain a stoic expression like the rest of them.

What could the woman possibly have against him? Yes, he partied, but he'd made sure to avoid scandals or anything that would bring their family name into disrepute. He performed all his royal obligations enthusiastically and successfully.

She would have to spell out her objections, right here in front of everyone.

Across the room, his birth mother, Queen Sapphire, met his gaze. The rigid line of her jaw indicated she wasn't pleased with the direction of the conversation. But the almost imperceptible nod she gave him showed she supported of his actions. And he was grateful.

Everyone else watched them, seemingly reluctant to interfere. Nevertheless, he had no requirement for anyone to come to his rescue. He could fight his own battles.

Queen Zulekha turned to the king, chin tilted. "In certain quarters, Azikiwe is referred to as 'the whore of Bagumi,' which makes him most unsuitable for the crown."

CHAPTER THREE

The fuck?

The loud, sharp inhalations from the other people in the throne room confirmed Zik had heard Queen Zulekha correctly.

The woman had just called him a whore.

Right to his face. In the presence of his mother, no less.

Never mind that Danai was here, too, along with Zawadi and the king.

"What…" Outspoken and eloquent, Zik was not usually the quiet sort. Nor was he the grin-and-bear-it type. However, he was too stunned to think coherently.

Instinct finally kicked in, and he fell into his natural mode, reading the room. His first rule of effective communication was to listen.

Except, no one spoke for a few seconds, and silence descended, only interrupted by the barely noticeable humming air-conditioners.

So, he resorted to the next best thing: studying the body language.

Danai looked downwards, not meeting anyone's gaze in apparent embarrassment, matching Zawadi's uneasy tug at his collar.

The tightness around Queen Sapphire's eyes and the flattened lips telegraphed her barely restrained wrath. Zik understood the family politics. She was the peacemaker, and she wouldn't disrespect the king. Not in such a public arena and in front of Zawadi's guest. Until their wedding, Danai was still an outsider and a commoner.

"Zulekha, is this true?" The king sounded vexed, rubbing the middle of his forehead with his knuckle, eyes closed. Not the first time he'd shown frustration where Zik was concerned. That Zik wasn't a model of morality like Zawadi.

Never mind Zawadi being the cause of this messy situation when he'd waltzed in here and announced he would abandon his fiancée and royal inheritance.

With the focus now directed at Zik, the attitude became frosty. Typical.

"Yes, it is, and Azikiwe knows it to be true," the first consort responded in a hard tone, her expression devoid of emotion.

"True?" Zik opened his mouth and let his indignation flow out, his grip on the armchair tightening. "O Truth Bearer, Heavens forbid we hear nothing but the truth from you."

"Mind your tone!" Queen Zulekha raised her voice, her haughty mask slipping, replaced by outrage tightening her already taut features.

Zik laughed dryly, shaking his head. The woman had just tried to shame him by calling him a whore in front of other people, and she dared to tell him to mind his tone? Not happening. She might be the king's consort, but he was the king's son. The king's blood.

He never went looking for fights. He would rather make love than make war. But bring the battle to him? Hurt someone he loved? Like the king's first wife had just done by trying to humiliate Zik publicly, hence, trying to humiliate Zik's mother in the same vein? And he would knock the person out. Damn right he would. He wasn't afraid of bloodying his knuckles, physically and metaphorically.

"Mother dearest, that ship has sailed. We are all truth-speakers now. So, here's a truth." He leaned forward, hands clasped together, elbows on knees. "The people who refer to me as the Whore of Bagumi are small-minded, judgemental, puritanical bigots who've probably never enjoyed anything in their pathetic lives and want everyone else to be miserable."

"Azikiwe!" his father scolded sharply, his disappointment evident in his stony expression.

Nothing new there. It just went to show the disparity in the way the two siblings were treated.

Zawadi dismantled a decades-old agreement and their father brushed it off without so much as a twitch. Meanwhile, Zik received disapproval because he wouldn't jump through the same hoops, and then he got insulted, as well.

"Papa, am I not telling the truth? Your wife says I'm unacceptable for the throne because of my personal life. Yet, when you were a young man, you did the same things. So isn't it hypocrisy when you became king and I can't—"

"That's enough!"

"Is it, Papa? Why am I even here when you obviously don't want me as Crown Prince?"

"Regardless of who becomes the future king," his father said in a stern voice, all joviality gone. "We need to salvage our relationship with the Onohs. We must fulfil the marriage contract, and you are the available son."

Zik's lungs constricted, and he struggled to breathe. His father might have slapped him, and the physical blow wouldn't hurt as much as the emotional punch of those words.

He wasn't here because he was suitable, or qualified, or good. He wasn't even here because they wanted him.

He'd been invited along only because he was unattached. Single. A bachelor. To clean up Zawadi's mess. Yes, he had a reputation for being 'the fixer' amongst his siblings. They came to him when they had a problem or needed something they couldn't acquire via other means. But this was taking the cake.

"So, if you had another single son, if Reb or Zed were single, you'd offer Amara to them instead?" A wonder he didn't choke on the words as his head drooped and his muscles weakened at the notion of his other siblings ending up with Amara.

"No! Over my dead body!" Queen Sapphire's vehement tone cut through the air like the brutal arc of a sword.

Zik lifted his head. He'd never heard his mother speak in such a tone in the king's presence, certainly not publicly. But the imperial tilt of Queen Sapphire's chin, her strong posture and calm focus showed she was determined to speak her mind.

"Azikiwe," she continued in a steady, low-pitched voice, her gaze locked onto him. "No one will bypass you and give your rights away to anyone else. Zawadi had his chance with Amara, and he blew it. Now, she's yours to claim. No one else's. No one will dare try it. I can promise you that. Of course, whether she'll want to marry into this family after the appalling way she's been treated is quite another matter."

She didn't do this, defying royal protocols and etiquette. Generally, in public arenas, Queen Zulekha was the voice of the two women except on occasions where she wasn't present. Yet, it didn't mean Zik's mother didn't communicate in other non-vocal ways. He had learned the art of visual expressions and reading body language through her.

So, her taking a vocal stance and defending him now overwhelmed him. Especially since neither his father nor Queen Zulekha seemed happy about it. A lump of emotion clogged his throat, and he swallowed hard. "Thank you, Mum."

His mother waved him off with a curt nod and turned towards his brother. "Zawadi, I'm glad you found love and happiness with Danai, and I wish only the best for both of you. However, you haven't gone about this the right way."

Okay. It seemed his mother wasn't quite done with voicing her opinions. For once today, Zik was glad the attention wasn't directed at him.

"You've been living in Somie with Danai for three months while engaged to Amara. Now, two months to your traditional marriage ceremony, you decide not to go through with it. Meanwhile, you haven't told Amara. She is a human with feelings, not a toy you can possess and dispose at your whim."

"Mum, I don't mean to hurt Amara." Zawadi bowed his head, looking regretful.

"I know you don't, son. But you're hurting her by making her the last to know. You should have told her the moment you realised you had feelings for someone else. She should have been the first to know. And you should have given her the opportunity of breaking things off with you, not the other way around."

Finally, someone calling out Zawadi's bullshit. But obviously, Queen Sapphire spoke from a place of love in correcting a bad behaviour rather than trying to shame or humiliate him, like Queen Zulekha had tried to do with Zik.

"Please accept my apologies, Mum. I will speak to Amara as soon as this meeting ends."

"Apology accepted. Go do it now. The rest of you, please excuse us. The old people would like to talk amongst ourselves," she said in an amused tone. "You should all stay for dinner. I insist."

She gave a pointed look at Zik which meant she knew he would have headed straight home as soon as he walked out of here.

But he nodded in acceptance of her command. With curt bows and "Your Majesty, Your Graces," he followed Zawadi and Danai out of the throne room.

"I need to call Amara," Zawadi said to Danai as soon as the double doors shut behind them.

Zik walked past them, heading down the corridor towards the side entrance.

"Zik, wait," Danai called out, her heels tapping against the marble floor as she hurried to him. "Are you okay?"

He barked out a cold laugh and tilted his head back. "No, I'm not okay. But it doesn't matter."

"It matters." Zawadi approached. "My mother shouldn't have said that to you."

"Why not?" he spat out with disdain. "She only said what the rest of you think about me, anyway."

"Zik—"

"Look, it's fine. I'll see you later." He cut his brother off and walked away.

He couldn't stay there and continue the conversation, mostly because as volatile as he felt, he didn't want to say anything to hurt his brother's feelings. He'd been disrespectful enough with his father in the throne room. He was at risk of being disowned or at the very least being stripped of his royal status already. He didn't want to alienate his siblings as well.

He knew enough about himself to accept he wouldn't do well without his family. He was not a loner. He needed his people. His friendship with Ejike and Ekene was probably in jeopardy due to

Zawadi breaking the engagement with Amara. They would be angry, which they had every right to be.

He ignored the staff and the bodyguards and took the stone path meandering through the gardens down towards the lake, where his mother found him about an hour later.

Zik stood on the shore of Lake Miri, staring at the golden shimmery reflection of the setting sun on the water. Warm sand squished between his toes, his jacket draped over his arm, his shoes in his hand.

He heard the rustle of fabric as she approached before she even spoke.

"I knew I'd find you here."

He smiled, shaking his head. "I couldn't very well disobey your order. Not if I want to live."

After she'd supported him, the least he could do was stay. Plus, he didn't want to risk being told off by her, not when she'd looked ready to pick a fight with anyone including the king.

She laughed softly, standing beside him, facing the lake. "Sometimes, you egotistical men need to be reminded where the power truly lies."

"Not me." He clutched his chest in mock hurt. "You don't think I'm egotistical, too?"

She giggled and patted his arm. "Yes, you as well. I've tried to raise you to not have an over-bloated sense of self. But I'm also aware that you are raised in a generation who feel entitled to everything. Add a royal title and money in the bank, and you think the world is yours to play with."

Trust his mother to give him a dose of reality. One of the many reasons he loved her.

"Talking about royal titles, have I lost mine?" he asked tentatively.

His title brought him a lot of privileges, and life would be challenging without it. But as long as he wasn't cut off from the family, he would survive.

"No. Your father needs you for the marriage contract. So, he wouldn't cut off his nose to spite his face," she replied in a sober tone. "However, you will apologise to him so the slate is wiped clean. Then we can revisit the issue of the future king at a later date when everyone is calmer."

The breath hitched in his throat. They couldn't put this matter to rest already because of …

"Does she really not want me to be Crown Prince? Am I so horrible?"

His mother sighed and pressed his forearm briefly. "No, you're not. Don't ever think that. But you must understand. The news of Zawadi's abdication is a terrible blow to Zulekha. All her life, she has looked forward to her first son becoming the future king. That's the reason she married your father, so her son could become king. And now, it looks like it's not going to happen. Coupled with the fact that she sees you as lesser than Zawadi. She believes in hierarchy. First wife. First son. Everyone else is secondary. So, it will take her a while to accept anyone else as crown prince but Zawadi. So be patient with her."

Could she ask for less, possibly?

"I don't know if I can. But I'll try." As long as the woman didn't continue to say nasty things about him, he was happy to live and let live. But there was still the other issue. "Mum, I don't know if I can marry Amara."

Her face furrowed. "Why? Is there someone else?"

He wished! It would be so much simpler then. That's how Zed had gotten out of an arranged marriage. Zawadi, too, for that matter.

"No. But wouldn't it be better to just set her free from the contract and let her go live her life free from obligations to her family and ours? It just seems unfair for us to shunt her from one brother to another. Like we're playing with her life or something."

His mother didn't speak for a while. Zik stood still waiting for her response.

"Remember, one of the holiday periods when Amara and her brothers came to spend time here. She'd gone swimming in the lake and got her feet caught on something underwater and was flailing. You jumped into the water and untangled her from the reed, saving her from drowning."

Instantly, he was teleported back to that August evening when he'd been sixteen. They'd been having a teen party on the beach with a bonfire and music. Osita, Ekene, Ejike, Zawadi, Kweku, and a few other friends had been there. Isha and Amara had tagged along and gone swimming in the lake. Amara had gotten into trouble, and Isha had called out for help. Zik had been first in the dark water, feeling around for what had caught Amara's leg. Spluttering, she'd clung onto him as he'd carried her out of the water.

He'd forgotten the memory, locked it away along with several others involving Amara to keep his sanity over the years once he'd realised she would wed his brother.

"Yes, I remember, Mum. But what has it got to do with anything?"

The queen gave him a wistful smile. "I brought it up because I need you to think about the marriage contract in the same vein. You will rescue Amara from the shame of your brother's rejection. She waited a long time to be wed to him, over a decade. She made arrangements, planned a wedding, invited her friends and family. Only for your brother to change his mind at the last minute. Think about what it would do to her self-esteem. And then, knowing you didn't even offer to step in for Zawadi would be worse. Because it's not just one brother rejecting her, it'll be two brothers."

His mother turned to him, reached up and cupped his cheeks with both palms, staring deep into his eyes. "I know that sometimes you feel unseen, unappreciated. But know that I see you and appreciate you. Many years ago, I asked you to make a sacrifice. Today, I'm asking you to make another one. Take your brother's place, offer to marry Amara. Save her from the shame."

"But ... She probably doesn't want me." The memory of Amara's last Twitter dig at him returned. The princess hated him, no doubt about it. She would never marry him.

"I know, son. The risk of being rejected is high. But do what your brother couldn't. Fix the mess Zawadi created. Give Amara the opportunity to reject you and say no to the marriage. Don't take that away from her. Please."

Expressed so distinctly, how could he say no to her request? He was the fixer, after all, wasn't he?

Bowing his head, Zik kissed the side of his mother's hand. "I'll do it."

CHAPTER FOUR

"I'm sorry but I'm in love with someone else."

Zawadi's words ricocheted in Amara's head as she stared at the engagement ring sitting on the wooden dressing table.

Screaming with rage, she'd flung it across the room during their video chat two days ago when he'd broken off their engagement. However, the cleaner had rescued it and placed it on her dressing table.

Now. the ring, the glare of the sparkling diamond, taunted her, and she wished she could fling it into the depths of the river of lava in Mordor, or better still, shove it down Zawadi's throat.

She would've done it, too, if he'd had the decency to meet her in person rather than from across the telephone network.

Yes, they all lived under a pandemic, but it wasn't an excuse for him not to have visited her in person to announce he was ending their relationship. The bloody coward!

Amara paced her bedroom, trying not to smash things or let the fury get the better of her, hands clenched by her sides. Over the past few days, her mood had swung from rage to despair and back again, a never-ending roller-coaster.

What did she do to deserve Zawadi abandoning her?

She'd known him for as long as she could remember. Their families had a friendly relationship which started way before she was born. She had childhood memories of them being in each other's homes. Therefore, he'd always been a big part of her life.

He'd been a young, aloof, untouchable, unattainable noble first son of a king who would one day become king himself. All the young girls in their circles—children of power brokers, politicians, industrial tycoons—had wanted him. She'd had her own innocent infatuations about him.

Then she'd found out that one day, she would marry him, and she'd revelled in knowing that he would be hers. She'd won the grand prize of the crown prince of the Kingdom of Bagumi.

Over the years, their relationship had evolved from him barely noticing her about ten years ago to him properly proposing to her last year. In the interim, they'd grown to know each other better.

Zawadi was disciplined and responsible, the kind of man she wanted. Even better, he wasn't a womaniser like his brother. Not that she wanted to think about *that one* right now. In all the Saene brotherhood, he'd seemed the most steadfast and reliable.

Point was, Zawadi had been the epitome of the man she wanted to spend the rest of her life with. Someone a woman could depend on, even if she wouldn't be able to actually lean on him as he didn't seem the cuddly kind. But he would've worked.

They were going to become a power couple. The best in Africa if not the world.

She'd felt untouchable. Invincible.

Until two days ago.

"Aaaaarrrrgggghhh!" She yelled her frustration yet again, fighting not to let the tears overwhelm her. She'd cried plenty already.

She'd waited ten years for him. Counted down the days to their wedding.

And then, Zawadi turned around to tell her he loved someone else. Just like that. Barely two months to their traditional marriage.

How could he do this to her? What did she do wrong? What could she have done better?

She'd been committed to him.

But he'd stopped loving her and had fallen in love with his bodyguard.

Amara had suspected something was going on the first time she'd met the Danai woman. The bodyguard had an attitude and had caused a ruckus with Amara's entourage all in the name of security protocols.

She hadn't wanted to suspect Zawadi. He'd given her no reasons previously to think he would become unfaithful to her.

Turned out she should have trusted her instincts and should have queried if something had been going on between him and the woman. Due to the pandemic lockdown, Zawadi and the protection officer had been living together in his country home. All the while he'd been talking to Amara on long-distance calls, he'd been having a cosy affair with his bodyguard.

Zawadi was as much of a dog as his brother Zik. At least Zik didn't hide it and pretend like Zawadi had done.

The most painful part of this humiliation? She'd planned a wedding and had invited everyone to what was supposed to be the event of the year.

For heaven's sake, she'd been planning a wedding, their future life together, while he'd been carrying on with his bodyguard!

Instead, now her meticulously planned life was a fiasco, and she nursed a heartbreak, to boot.

Her phone pinged with a calendar reminder for a meeting with her mother and Zawadi's mother to resolve the problem caused by Zawadi.

Enraged about the annulment of the engagement, her father had called the Bagumian king and demanded they fulfil the marriage contract. The two monarchs had had a long conversation in which Zawadi had joined to apologise.

Now, she assumed Queen Zulekha wanted to apologise to her mother, too.

Amara checked her appearance in the full-length mirror and smoothed down her maxi-length black and gold silk dress, fluffed the hair she'd pulled into a high ponytail, and made sure her make-up was perfect. She wasn't about to let

Zawadi's mother see her looking less than perfect. She wanted the woman to see what her son would miss out on.

Many would have a field day about her broken engagement. The journalists and social media would have a frenzy.

But she would not let anyone see her fall from grace.

Yesterday, she'd posted 💔 on her Twitter account. Of course, that had spawned a lot of speculations. She'd had to mute the Tweet as thousands reacted to it.

However, she'd checked this morning and found a Tweet from Azikiwe's account @playerzik: *Where do broken hearts go?*

She'd known immediately it had been a reference to her post. At first, she'd wondered if he'd been mocking her, and she'd been furious. Then she'd remembered her dig at him a few days ago when she'd seen a picture of him with a woman when he'd gone to a friend's funeral over the weekend.

For years, they'd been trolling each other's accounts, taking swipes at each other. But this time, she wasn't even sure how to feel about the 'Where do broken hearts go?' tweet.

Warmth had spread through her chest. Was he trying to be sympathetic?

No. Not Zik. He was being rude, as usual. She shouldn't ever cut him any slack, especially after what his brother had done to her. They were all birds of the same feather.

Fighting another bout of fury, Amara left her bedroom, high-heeled sandals clicking against the hard flooring as she sashayed down the corridor of Onicha Palace. She'd come home at the start of the lockdown to be with her parents. Her job as the director of marketing for BrightComm headed by her oldest brother Osita was being wrapped up. Because of her scheduled move to Bagumi after the marriage to Zawadi, she was transitioning and training her deputy to take over the position after she left. All of it was up in the air now. Damn Zawadi.

She entered the reception room where a technician connected the audio-visual equipment in readiness for the video conference. She knocked and walked into her mother's private quarters. An assistant feathered a powder brush over the queen's makeup.

"Amara, *kedu*? How are you feeling today?"

Her mother, Lolo Egoyibo Onoh, stood, waving the assistant away. Many referred to Amara as her copy. She approached Amara, placing hands on her shoulders to look her over. Queen Ego, as the populace referred to her, wore one of her formal gowns in turquoise lace with coral trinkets, a beaded crown, and a white horse tail whisk in her hand.

Seeing the flurry of activities in the next room and knowing she would be facing a member of Zawadi's family, the despair clawed its way back up Amara's throat, making tears back up behind her eyelids. All she could manage was a resigned shrug. "I don't know, Mum. Do I have to do this?"

Her mother slid her arms around her shoulders and pulled her into a hug. "Nwa m, of course not. You don't have to do anything you don't want to. I can speak to Azikiwe's mother myself."

Amara jerked back, glancing up. "Zik's mother? I thought this meeting was with Zawadi's mother."

The regal Queen Zulekha had been her point of contact in the Bagumi royal family. She'd been the one in discussions with Queen Ego and Amara about the wedding preparations.

"Yes, it was at first. When your father spoke to King Ibrahim yesterday, they agreed the first queen would call me. However, last night, Sapphire messaged me to say she would be the one on the video call today. Is there a problem?"

"No. It's just that I've never really spoken one-to-one with Zik's mother. I mean, I've always interacted with Queen Zulekha at public events and privately. So why wouldn't Zawadi's mother want to talk to me herself now?"

"Well, they are both from the same family. At this stage, I don't think it matters too much which of them is at the meeting. The important thing is what they have to say and how they will rectify this problem."

"That's true." She wanted to know how they would solve the problem of Zawadi marrying another woman. Amara would not share him with someone else. Although Zawadi's father had two wives. "Mummy, do you think they are going to suggest that I allow Zawadi to take a second wife while I become the first?"

Her mother frowned. "As far as I know, nobody has mentioned Zawadi having two wives. Is this something you would consider?"

"Of course not. I can't even imagine sharing my husband with another woman." She shuddered.

"But you know King Ibrahim has two wives, so it's something they accept in their family."

"Mummy, mba o. I don't accept it. I am better off on my own."

"Ngwanu, let's forget it," the queen said, and they walked back into the reception room. "Are you people ready?"

"Yes, Your Highness," the lead technician replied. "We just need to attach the microphone and earpiece for you."

Amara and her mother settled on the same sofa, facing a large screen and a camera. The team proceeded to clip the wireless speaker-microphone earpieces and performed sound checks.

Minutes later, the screen went from a blank to showing the close-up image of Queen Sapphire, hair wrapped in a stylish yellow turban with a row of sapphires embedded in front, face made-up impeccably. Her beauty and elegance shone through the grainy internet connection.

"Good afternoon," Queen Ego said.

"Good afternoon, Your Grace," Amara added, unsure why her heart raced at the sight of the Bagumian queen.

"Good afternoon," Queen Sapphire replied with a warm smile. "It's so good to see both of you. Thank you for agreeing to meet with me, especially after what has happened." She placed her right hand on her chest, the white tips of her manicured fingers visible. "Please let me say with all my heart and on behalf of my family that I am truly sorry for what has happened."

The woman sounded sincere, and Amara swallowed the lump in her throat. "Thank you, Your Grace."

"Amara, how are you coping?" Queen Sapphire asked.

She glanced at her mother, remembering she was supposed to keep it together. "I'm doing as well as can be under the circumstances."

The Bagumian royal nodded. "I've been thinking about you over the past few days. I know it's a big blow to you, especially so close to your wedding date, but try and stay strong. This is only a blip in your life. I know you may not see it now, but you have a wonderful future."

"Thank you for your kind words." Amara glanced at her mother again.

"Yes, we appreciate the efforts you are making," her mother said. "But I can't tell you enough how disappointed we are at Zawadi's behaviour, considering our families have had a strong relationship over the years. I thought he respected us, but the way he treated Amara was wrong."

"I know that, and trust me, Zawadi has felt my displeasure about his actions. He understands he was wrong," Queen Sapphire said.

The mention of Zawadi's name made Amara's anger boil, and she spoke before thinking it through. "But Your Grace, it's not just enough that he understands what he did wrong. There has to be some consequences."

"Amara!" her mother scolded.

"What?" she retorted. "It's true. He can't just get away with it. Doesn't the marriage contract state that I get to marry the crown prince?" Her mother tugged her arm, a sign for Amara to be cautious, but she ignored her and carried on. "So, if Zawadi doesn't marry me, he doesn't get to be the crown prince."

"Oh, okay." Queen Sapphire nodded. "Would Zawadi stepping down as Crown Prince make you happy?"

"Yes, Your Grace. It would."

"Therefore, I can take it that you consent to marrying Azikiwe, then."

Wait. What? Amara's heart slammed into her chest. That wasn't where she thought this conversation was going. Marrying Zik? She shook her head.

"Pardon? I don't understand," she replied, trying to calm her racing heart.

"Let me explain. If Zawadi steps down as Crown Prince, that means Azikiwe automatically becomes the Crown Prince, and since he is single, he is available to fulfil the marriage contract with you. Are you willing to marry Azikiwe?"

Amara's cheeks flamed hot. How did she not think about this? Did she just walk into a trap with her eyes open?

"I..." She opened her mouth, but nothing came out, and she looked at her mother hoping the woman would save her.

"I think we need time to think about this new offer," Queen Ego said.

"Of course, I understand," Queen Sapphire replied. "I just wanted to let you know this option is available. Azikiwe has consented to marry Amara, and if she's in agreement, we can proceed as originally planned with the wedding arrangements. The only difference will be the groom. Amara, I want you to know that I would love for you to be my daughter-in-law and the future queen of Bagumi."

Amara gasped. The woman was really on the charm offensive. No wonder she'd come to the meeting instead of Queen Zulekha. She'd come to woo Amara on behalf of her son. "Thank you, Your Grace."

"You're welcome. And another thing. Please give us your decision, either way, by the end of tomorrow. We are scheduled to issue a statement on Friday so we'll need your answer before then."

That left Amara with only twenty-four hours to decide. "Noted."

"My regards to the king and everyone else. Have a good evening."

"Same to you."

"Bye."

The call ended, and the screen returned to blue.

"Mum, what just happened?" Amara turned, still struggling to process the video call.

"You had a marriage proposal." Her mother beamed a smile.

"From Zik." She rumpled her face. "I don't want to marry Zik, of all people."

"What's wrong with him?" Her mother looked confused.

She would not understand—she just saw the charming son of a king.

But Amara knew the truth. Zik was a man-whore, a fuck boy, although she would never use those phrases to describe him to her mother.

"He's a womaniser. There's a photo of him with a different woman practically every week."

Her mother laughed. "Is that what you're worried about? He's a young man who is single. He can play the field if he wants. But when he gets married, he'll settle down."

Amara jumped off the sofa and rubbed her hand over her face. "How do you know, Mum? There are many men who cheat when they are married. I don't think I can do this."

"Okay," her mother replied in a solemn tone. "We can reject the offer, and it shouldn't be a big deal since they reneged on the marriage contract first with Zawadi. However, you should bear in mind that Azikiwe will become the Crown Prince, marry someone else, and she will become the future queen of Bagumi. Do you really want to give away this opportunity for something you've been waiting for all your adult life? Just think about it."

CHAPTER FIVE

"Isha, how are you?" Amara said when she answered the phone call later that evening while sitting up against the pillows in her bed.

"I'm doing great. How about you? I heard about what happened. I'm so sorry about Zawadi," her best friend said. They hadn't seen each other for a while. Not since her brother Zediah's and his wife Riona's baby shower about four months ago. It had become more difficult to see each other since Isha's husband Zain became president of Wanai.

"It's been a few tough days, but I'm doing a little better today. I spoke to your mother about three hours ago," she replied, remembering the video chat with the queen.

"I know. She called me, too, and told me what happened this evening. That's why I'm calling. I didn't know. Why didn't you tell me?"

"I was too distraught at first. I didn't really want to talk to anyone. Then of course, I know you have your hands full with a country to govern and raising two young children. How are Ifeh and Nadia doing?"

"It's been challenging, especially with home-schooling an eleven-year-old boy and a six-year-old girl. Hopefully, the schools will reopen for the new academic year in September, and we can have some level of normalcy. Still, you should've called me as soon as this happened. You know I'll always make time for you."

Her heart warmed a little. "I know. You've always been there for me. But this was a little different. Zawadi is your brother. I wasn't sure if you knew that he was seeing someone else all along."

"Me. Never. You should know me better than that. If I'd known there was something going on between him and Danai all along, I would have made him tell you immediately. I wouldn't keep such a thing secret."

Relief rushed through her, even though she'd known Isha wouldn't do wrong by her. "I realise it now, and I'm sorry for doubting our friendship."

"It's not a problem. I can understand why you would feel that way. So how are you handling it, seriously?"

A sigh escaped her. "I have my good and bad moments. I switch between wanting to scream, to wanting to cry. But since your mum called, I've been panicking a little."

"Panicking? Why?"

Amara lowered her voice, although no one else was in the room, the door shut. "Because she proposed to me on behalf of Zik."

"Is that good or bad?" Isha sounded confused.

Not the answer she'd been expecting. "Well, I don't know. This is Zik we're talking about."

"But you know Zik. What's the problem?"

"That's exactly the problem. I *know* him. He's Player Zik. Playboy Prince Extraordinaire."

"Oh, come on. You make him sound like a cardboard cut-out or just a one-dimensional stereotype."

Outrage filled her this time. "But that's what he is—one-dimensional. He's a womaniser who's only interested in his next fling."

"Woah. You sound as if you really don't like him."

Amara sucked in a deep breath. "I'm sorry. I forgot he's your brother. He just winds me up so much, I don't even understand it sometimes."

"What exactly does he do to wind you up?"

Should she roll out the full list? "For starters, he trolls me on social media."

Isha laughed. "More like you two troll each other. I've seen you sub-tweeting him several times. The two of you are as bad as each other on there."

Amara's cheeks heated, and she spluttered. Isha was correct. Amara gave as good as she got, maybe sometimes even worse than Zik ever did to her.

"For someone you supposedly dislike so much, it looks like you stalk him on social media instead of avoiding him or blocking him," Isha continued.

"Anyway, it doesn't matter." Her friend was right again. She would admit to trolling Zik on purpose. It seemed she needed the social media war for some excitement or something. Amara tried to change the subject. "How are things in Wanai?"

"Honey, I know you're trying to change the subject. But I didn't call you about Wanai. I called you about you. If getting married to Zik sounds like a bad idea, you can reject the proposal. No one will hold it against you, especially in this situation. The two of you haven't had time to date, so it's only fair for you to have doubts. But honestly, Zik is more than what he's portrayed in the media. Yes, he's my brother, and I'm biased. But he is generous and compassionate, sensitive and considerate, protective and loyal."

"Hang on. Are we talking about the same person here? Sensitive and loyal? This is a man who behaves as if he's God's gift to women and changes partners so frequently. How can he be loyal to anyone?"

"Seriously? How can you say that? Have you forgotten those days at uni when we used to practically start our periods at the same time and we'd need someone to go and get some toiletries for us? We'd send him a text, and he would turn up with tampons and everything we needed, including those cupcakes we loved so much."

"Oh, yeah. He did that." Warmth bloomed through Amara as the memories came rushing back. "He would make sure we had painkillers and comfort food."

"Exactly. And when things turned bad between me and Zain in those days, he stood by me during some really dark times."

"Yes, I remember." Amara sighed. "But being a great brother doesn't mean he'll be a great husband."

"True. I guess part of the problem is both of you never dated. So, you don't how each other behaves in private. And the current pandemic makes it difficult to meet regularly. Also, there is a time limit as the traditional wedding date is coming soon."

"Yes, I guess it's the reason I'm panicking. I don't want to feel trapped in the marriage if I find out later I can't live with him."

The line stayed silent for a few seconds before Isha spoke again. "How about adding a getting-to-know-you period to the marriage contract, allowing the two of you to spend time together and get to know each other? When the period ends and things don't work out, you can both walk away without any penalties. And you can both say you tried to make it work. Our parents would understand and let you be."

"Is that possible?" Amara asked, as her heart raced. This might be a solution to the problem.

Isha had made some valid point about the Zik of their younger days. He'd been sensitive and considerate. But Zik's current reputation as a playboy eclipsed all else. Amara wouldn't permanently tie herself to a man who wouldn't commit to her. The trial period would give her a get-out clause and some peace of mind.

"Yes, it is. I'll talk to Zik about it. But I don't see it being a problem."

"Okay. Let's do that."

"Does that mean you're saying yes to Zik if there's a trial period?"

Was she? Amara's heart jolted.

Talking to Isha had given her a measure of reassurance about Zik. However, there were other issues. Like a decade of being groomed as the future queen of Bagumi and the humiliation of not becoming one if she turned down this proposal. Honestly, Zik being the crown prince was the only reason she would even sniff at him. And the Royal House of Saene owed her, darn it!

"Yes," she blurted out. "But I have a few other conditions."

"Oh. Okay." Isha sounded cheerful. "Do you want to tell me what they are?"

Her cheeks heated. "No. They're personal. Is it possible to get Zik's phone number so I can chat with him directly?"

"Of course. I'll message it to you right away."

"Great. And thank you so much for calling. I should have called you earlier."

"I told you not to worry about it. Just take it easy. And let me know as soon as you make a decision. No matter what it is, you're still my bestie and my sister."

"Thank you. I appreciate it."

"I've got to run. I need to make sure the kids are in bed. Talk soon. My love to Mummy and the boys."

"My love to Zain and the kids. Bye."

Amara's phone pinged as soon as the call ended with a text from Isha containing Zik's number.

Her mouth dried out and her chest lightened as she saved the number in her contacts. She probably should wait a while and compose her thoughts before sending him a message.

But she had only a few hours left to decide, and she wanted clarifications to certain things before she could make up her mind.

So, she sat on her bed and started typing:

Hi, Zik. This is Amara. I spoke to your mother earlier today and she told me of your proposal. I have some questions and conditions before I can decide.

She pressed send. A few seconds later, a message pinged back.

Amara, this is a pleasant surprise. I'm happy to answer any questions you have. So, shoot.

Adrenaline rushed through her, and she sent another one.

The first thing is more a condition than a question. If I agree to marry you, then you promise not to have sex with any other person for the duration of our marriage starting from when you get my agreement.

A response popped in almost instantly.

You're damned right, babygirl. I don't share. If you say yes to me, you say no to everyone else.

The first half of the message had her heart rate skyrocketing and heat pooling between her legs. Why the hell did she find that sexy? Yet, the last sentence was bloody annoying.

😠😠😠 You really are an arrogant SOB. I was referring to you being faithful to me and you turned it around and made it about you.

Babygirl, this is marriage. What's good for the goose is good for the gander. You can't expect me to be faithful to you and not give the same courtesy to me.

He was correct, but still infuriating that he managed to flip the conversation.

I'm not the one who sleeps around with different people all the time.

Maybe not. But since we're talking about sexual partners, how many have you had?

Piss off. It's none of your business. 😠

Isn't this something I should know as your husband-to-be? 🙁

I haven't said yes, yet.

Fair enough.

Anyway, are you going to be faithful or not?

Yes, Amara. I promise to be faithful to you if you agree to marry me.

Her breath hitched. Another surprise. She'd thought he would evade the question or try to make a smart remark like he'd done earlier. But the tone sounded serious, and he seemed to mean it. Would he keep to his word, though? She had no reasons to doubt him. Didn't know if he'd ever cheated on any previous lovers. All she had to go on were speculations and online gossip, which weren't reliable.

Isha had said Zik was loyal, and she trusted her friend. So, she would accept his word for now.

Okay, **she typed and sent.**

Good. Do you promise to do the same? To be faithful to me?

What was this? Why would he even ask her this question? Her first response was to start typing a retort. But she paused and took a deep breath. He'd answered her question solemnly. It was only fair for her to give him an honest reply without attitude. So, she backspaced, erasing what she'd previously written before starting again.

Yes, I promise to be faithful to you if we get married.

Thank you.

His reply made her heart skip a beat and caught her off balance. This Zik seemed different from the one she interacted with online. The one online seemed to only care about the banter. This one seemed to care about her feelings, which couldn't be right. This was *Zik*. He had to be playing a game with her. She couldn't predict his actions or responses, which left her on edge. She hesitated before typing:

I have another condition.

Go ahead.

I want you to undertake several health checks and tests—genotypes, HIV, STD, and others.

Done. But you must do the same tests too.

WTH. You can't be serious.

I'm dead serious. You will undergo the same tests as you demand from me. I need to go now but I look forward to your response tomorrow. Sweet dreams, babygirl.

Amara read his text, chucked her phone on the bed, and screamed in frustration. Who the hell did the bloody man think he was?

63

CHAPTER SIX

"Prince Azikiwe, how does it feel to be in the running for the future king of Bagumi?" the reporter asked in a monotone voice.

"It is an honour to be considered suitable to lead our great kingdom." Zik crooked his brow as he gave the standard response which had been prepared for him by the palace press coordinator and his own assistant, Lucas Bene, who stood to the side. He'd said that line so many times today, he was beginning to feel robotic and bored.

A sheaf of papers adorned with the royal logo sat on the table in case he needed them for reference to answer any questions. Also, the reporter could only ask a specific list of questions.

He was used to responding to media questions on the spur of the moment. But his life had changed since Zawadi's abdication. Now, his interactions with the media must be scripted for the most part.

Zik usually had a good relationship with paparazzi. His life had always been a source of curiosity for the rest of the world, and he indulged them when possible. He was not camera shy. If someone wanted to take a photo of him, he would pose for them. If someone asked him a question, he would answer from the heart. He was not used to having his guard up as high as was now expected of him. It proved stifling.

So surely, this man knew his current responses were canned and prepared. Not Zik at all. Yet, he didn't complain or probe to go more in-depth.

Outside, the stunning view of Regents Avenue and the city bathed in golden light as the sun descended towards the mountains in the distance gave the backdrop.

The panorama tempted him. He would rather be out there than be in here being interviewed by a reporter. But this was his new life, stuck in the Safari room of Darusa Palace dealing with press.

After the argument with his father on the day Zawadi had presented Danai, Zik had apologised. The king had accepted the apology and had ordered him to "get married, settle down, clean up your act, prove that you can rule a kingdom, and then perhaps you can become king one day."

So Zik had spent most of today dealing with reporters. He'd done television interviews earlier on the day. This man was the designated royal correspondent from the national newspapers, Bagumi Today, and would be the last for the day. The interviews would run tomorrow, along with the official announcement from King Ibrahim about Zawadi stepping down as Crown Prince.

Zik picked up the glass of water on the table and took a sip, wishing it was something stronger.

Less than a week into the new position as the Interim Crown Prince and he wasn't altogether enamoured with it. For one, the position was temporary while the issue of the succession was discussed and resolved. Which meant uncertainty. Yet, he had all the responsibilities and restrictions associated with the title. Not fun at all.

Except for the small window last night, when he'd been in the car, heading from Beya Castle to Darusa Palace while exchanging text messages with Amara.

His chest tightened, and his breathing accelerated.

She still hadn't responded to his marriage proposal, and it was over twenty-four hours since his mother had made the offer. He'd been checking his phone for messages all day. Now he eyed it, praying for a notification. Something. Anything. Even a rejection would do. Just so he could get over this limbo and the churning in his gut.

Why he was so invested in her response, he couldn't fathom.

He shouldn't care. She'd been poised to marry his brother up until a few days ago. It shouldn't matter if she agreed to marry him now. He'd managed to live for many years knowing she would end up with someone else.

Perhaps his father's ultimatum to get married and settle down if he wanted to become the future king exacerbated the situation. Amara was available, eager to become a future queen, and acquainted with his family. She would make a suitable wife.

Nevertheless, he wouldn't lie to himself. The idea of being king didn't excite him as much as the idea of having Amara as his wife.

Hence his current anxiety like the teenage boy who'd entertained fantasies of marrying the princess once upon a time.

Shit. Since the conversation with his mother by the lakeside days ago, he'd been flooded with resurrected teen memories.

The journalist shuffled his papers, drawing Zik's attention.

"You have a reputation of a party animal, enjoying the opulence and lifestyle that goes with it. Now that you are the interim crown prince with the possibility of becoming the future king, are you going to settle down and take a wife soon?"

The question prompted Zik to glance at his phone again, and the corner of his lips tipped up. He wasn't like Zawadi who had been trained from birth to repress and hide his emotions. Yes, the mantle of crown prince was stifling and the burden heavy as he was beginning to discover. However, he would take the moments available to be himself where possible.

So, for the first time today, he went off script. "As a matter of fact, I am ready to rise with the privilege of the crown prince. As such, I *am* looking to settle down as soon as possible, and I proposed to a certain lady. Right now, I'm waiting for her answer."

The reporter's eyes widened and brightened. He glanced around the room as if he didn't believe Zik, guessing he had gone off-script. "Are you serious, Your Highness?"

Zik grinned. "Of course I'm serious."

At the periphery of his vision, Lucas, his assistant, moved forward. But Zik waved him away, knowing what the man would say. Zik should stay on-script. However, the cat was out of the bag.

"Who is this lady? Can we know her name?" The reporter readied his pen and pad, although a voice recorder sat on a stand between them.

Zik chuckled. "Of course, I can't tell you her name yet. Not until I get a positive response."

"Of course." The reporter laughed.

Just then, Zik's phone vibrated on the table, and he grabbed it. "Excuse me."

He shouldn't interrupt the interview to check his phone. It was unprofessional. But his apprehension had gone through the roof. It seemed to be a Twitter notification. He'd set his phone to notify him every time Amara tweeted. It seemed she'd done so.

He pressed his thumb on the biometric scanner, swiped to read the tweet, and a huge grin spread on his face as giddy relief flooded him.

Her tweet read: *I said yes!*

His gaze went heavenward, and he exhaled a huge breath.

Although he wasn't tagged or mentioned in the tweet, he knew it was addressed to him, same as all her other subtweets. The woman, though. She hadn't sent him a message directly. Instead, she'd posted it online as per usual. They really had to talk about her method of communication.

Still, he would respond to show he'd seen it. He opened a new tweet and typed out: *She said yes!* 😀

This would cause a lot of speculation online before the formal statements and interviews were issued tomorrow.

"Your Highness, is that the answer you were expecting?" the reporter asked.

"Yes, it is. She said yes to my proposal. So I'm happy to inform you about my engagement to Princess Amara Onoh."

The reporter gasped, looking confused. "Congratulations, Your Highness. Is the princess not the same woman who was engaged to your brother?"

Zik had been prepared for this question, funnily enough by the palace press coordinator. So although the mention of Amara's engagement to Zawadi hit him in the solar plexus, he pushed through the hurt and didn't lose his cool.

"Zawadi left the princess broken-hearted when he ended their engagement. Amara is free to marry whomever she chooses, and she accepted my proposal. She is my fiancée now. If we're done here, I have a call to make."

"Of course, Your Highness. Thank you for your time, Prince Azikiwe." The man bowed.

Zik nodded and headed towards the door. Lucas stayed in the room to usher the journalist out while his lead bodyguard followed him along the corridors as he strode to his mother suite.

He typed out an SMS and sent it direct to Amara.

Babygirl, you're mine now.

It wasn't even five seconds before a reply came back.

You wish.

He chuckled aloud and sent:

You said yes.

Another one pinged.

Yes, I did. But you still have to come here and pay my bride price before you can claim me as yours.

The base of his spine tingled, and his pulse skyrocketed at the image of claiming her.

I look forward to it. Two months and counting down, babygirl.

Whatever.

Shaking his head, he chuckled and tucked the phone into his back pocket. He loved riling her up and getting a rise out of her. Hopefully, life with her would be fun.

The guard outside announced him before Zik walked into the reception room where his mother sat on a settee, ending a phone call.

"Have you heard, Mum? She said yes!" He couldn't hide the excitement in his voice as he sat on the sofa beside her.

She pulled him into a hug, a smile curling her lips. "I know, son. Her mother just called me. It's wonderful news. How do you feel?"

She looked up at his face.

He hadn't stopped grinning since reading Amara's tweet. "I haven't slept properly the last few days. So, I'm relieved and pleased."

"I'm relieved and pleased, too. She left it so late, I thought she would reject it. I wouldn't have blamed her, though."

Zik nodded. "Honestly, Mum. You made it possible. I don't think she would've accepted my proposal if you hadn't intervened directly. Thank you."

He hugged her again. This was nowhere near how he thought he would make a marriage proposal or receive a response. Not by proxy through his mother. However, he now understood some of the merits of family elders negotiating arranged marriages.

"You're welcome," Queen Sapphire said. "I'm so excited. I get to be the mother of the groom, at last."

The two of them laughed.

But Zik knew the fairy tale ending was still a long way off.

CHAPTER SEVEN

One week and counting down.

Amara stared at the tweet she'd posted yesterday. It had over ten thousand likes, and retweets. Thousands of people quote-tweeting her because she'd restricted who could reply to her emails to those mentioned or those she followed.

Since the announcement about her engagement to Prince Azikiwe Saene, hordes of trolls had descended on her social media accounts.

She usually had trolls attacking her online anyway. A horrible part of the celebrity life these days. However, it seemed the news of her engagement to Zik brought a whole new level of hatred and vitriol from people who seemed to think they had a chance with the prince. Deluded bitches.

Anyway, today, the trolls weren't her headache as she'd started muting her social media posts. However, over the past few weeks, she and Zik had established a social media dialogue. When he posted something, she would subtweet it immediately and vice versa. Whenever he posted, she would receive a notification.

However, he hadn't responded to her recent tweet yesterday. She'd been on his profile wondering if she'd missed the notification, but his last tweet had been about a week ago. How unlike him not to subtweet her. Or at least send her an SMS, which he hadn't done either.

Should she text him? The only time she'd messaged him directly was in response to him or when she had questions relating to the upcoming traditional wedding. And although they had an amicable agreement to wed each other, they were doing it out of obligation to their families. Zik was getting a suitable royal wife in preparation for being the future king, and she was getting a crown prince for a husband as promised to her.

They made a good royal match. Full stop.

She wasn't foolish enough to believe there would be more. She'd trusted Zawadi to be faithful and to love her, and she'd been disappointed. She trusted Zik even less. If she couldn't rely on Zawadi, she definitely couldn't rely on Zik.

Sure Zik was charming, and he'd made her smile a few times over the past few weeks. Yet, a sense of humour didn't cover for the annoying moments

Best not to attempt to invest any depth of feelings into their relationship. Over the coming years, they would get used to each other. As long as he didn't cheat on her. She would never tolerate an unfaithful spouse, not even to become queen.

Still, she couldn't shake the unease about Zik not responding to her tweet. She'd become used to his subtweets and looked forward to them. There was comfort in knowing he read her posts and took time to respond.

Was he having second minds about their upcoming wedding? Zawadi had changed his mind at close to the last minute. Zik was likely to do the same, too.

Lord. Her body temperature went from hot to cold. Her stomach churned, and she clutched it, bending over. The thought of another man ditching her so spectacularly plagued her with nightmares already. She needed to know what was going on, otherwise she wouldn't sleep tonight.

She scrolled through to her brother Ekene's number and sent a message.

Have you got a minute to talk?

She liked to text Ekene first instead of calling him, especially at this time of night. Once, she'd called him in the evening, and he'd answered the phone while he'd been in the middle of having sex. Just gross. She'd screamed at him. He'd laughed and insisted he'd had to answer because whenever she called him, she was in some high drama situation she classed as an emergency since she was more a texter than a caller.

Still, she'd been so grossed, she now stuck to sending messages.

Her phone started ringing like she knew it would, and she tapped to connect.

"Lil' sis, ke kwanu? What's up?" her brother said.

Amara rolled her eyes at her brother's teasing. These days, she didn't bother to remind her brothers they didn't have a 'Big Sis' although they'd designated her as 'Lil'.

"Gi na Zik ekwugo nso-nso?" She resorted to Igbo which was the language she and her brothers spoke to each other privately, asking if he'd spoken to Zik recently.

"Yes, we are online right now playing GTA5," he replied equally in their local tongue. "My boy needed to blow off some steam after everything going on."

"You mean you guys are still playing right now?" Had Zik been playing online games with his friends instead of responding to her tweet? And she'd been here worried something happened to him. That would teach her to bother.

"Yes. I just grabbed my phone to talk to you," Ekene said. "Do you want me to call you back later?"

"No. It's just a quick chat." She didn't mind continuing the conversation with her brother in Igbo because Zik wouldn't be able to understand them anyway. "Did you say something happened to him?"

"You know his father's illegitimate son showed up?"

"Yes, I know."

"Well, the guy is contesting to become crown prince since he's older than Zik."

"Are you serious?"

Soon after Zawadi's abdication, King Ibrahim had introduced Kalahari as the lost son he'd had through one of the palace employees years ago. Isha had told Amara about the new prince, but no one had mentioned the possibility of the man becoming crown prince.

"Of course I'm serious," Ekene replied. "Can you imagine how we would feel if Pops introduced some guy to us as our brother and told Osita the person would inherit the crown instead of him. There will be problems o."

"Big problems," she concurred. None of them needed this complication. "Will Zik step down as crown prince because Kalahari is older? Will Kalahari become the future king?"

"I don't really know. All I know is that Zik is frustrated with the uncertainty."

Oh, Lord. What did all this mean? The panic returned, and Amara's chest tightened along with her fear of being jilted again by her fiancé. She rocked in place, hand holding the phone and trembling. Zawadi's scorn had traumatised her. Now, any sign of trouble sent her into heightened anxiety.

"I can imagine. Do you know if Zik wants to cancel the wedding?" she asked.

"No. Why do you think so?" Her brother sounded concerned.

"It's just that if the crown prince position gets taken away from Zik, then he may not need to marry me. He might withdraw the proposal. Will I have to marry his new brother instead?" She shuddered at the thought of having to do this all over. She was getting used to the idea of being with Zik and had accepted to marry him.

The whole thing had been stressful enough. She wouldn't repeat the process.

"No. Lil' sis, stop worrying. Your Igbankwu is in a week and it's happening, come rain or shine. Zik will not fail you. So, no shaking."

"Okay," she said, but wasn't convinced. She hadn't thought Zawadi would fail her, but he'd done so.

"You know what? I'll tell Zik to call you as soon as we get off this game."

"Okay. Thanks."

"No wahala. I should be home in a few days to help finalise the preparations. My sister is get-ting mar-ried," he said in a jovial singing tone.

Amara laughed. "I'll see you soon. Good night."

She hung up and scrubbed a palm over her face, debating whether to speak to her mother about the new situation with Zik. But then, she decided to leave it until tomorrow since her mother was probably in bed.

Still unsettled and unsure why even though she knew Zik was okay, she sent him a text.

I know you're still playing an online game with Ekene. But I heard about the situation with Kalahari wanting to be crown prince. Are you okay?

It was over a minute before a response came through.

I've been better.

Oh. Has a decision been made?

Why do you want to know?

I'm concerned about you.

You're concerned about me? You're taking the piss.

Why are you being rude? I'm trying to be nice.

You nice? You know I heard your conversation with Ekene, right?

Her cheeks flamed. How?

Oh. You understand Igbo?

My best friends are Igbo. Of course I understand it.

Shit. She should've realised it. Now, she scrambled for how to deflect him.

Well, I was having a conversation with my brother. You shouldn't eavesdrop on people. It's rude.

If I'm rude, what does that make you? Why pretend you're concerned about me? Aren't you more concerned about whether you made the right decision about marrying me?

His words came too close to the truth. She'd never been sure about marrying him. Also, she'd been concerned for him losing the crown prince title, not just for self-interest. But he didn't even appreciate her concern. That would teach her for caring. Frustrated and conflicted, she typed a hasty response.

Maybe I made the wrong decision.

She sent the message, blocked his number, and flopped on the bed, pounding the pillows.

***

'Maybe I made the wrong decision.'

Zik's hand trembled, and he dropped the phone on the floor after reading the text message from Amara. His stomach hardened, and he shot to his feet, discarding the headphones. He'd already abandoned the online game once he'd started exchanging messages with Amara this evening.

He grabbed the phone again, read the text to make sure he'd seen correctly. No change.

She'd actually sent those words to him.

Did she mean it? Would she consider rejecting his proposal in favour of his newest brother?

Fuck. He wasn't letting it happen. Enough of this text messaging. He would call her and hear her say it.

He pressed the button to dial her number and nothing happened. The call went nowhere. No ringing tone.

He checked again and redialled. No connection.

Okay. What happened there? Her network couldn't be down.

He grabbed his headset, re-joined the game chatroom and connected to Ekene's profile.

"Dude, what happened? You just disappeared from the game," Ekene said.

"Sorry. I was talking with your sister," he said. "We got cut off. Can you call her and check if her phone is dead or something?"

"Sure." There was a rustling sound as Ekene grabbed his phone. Then a ringing tone filled his ear. The phone rang several times then cut off. Then a beeping sound for a notification. "Dude. She didn't answer, but she sent a text to say she'll call me later."

"No problem. Thanks. I'll catch you later." Zik removed the headset and redialled Amara's number. There was no ringtone like when her brother called. As if the number didn't exist.

There could only be one reason. She'd blocked his phone number.

What the fuck!

What game was she playing? She was *his* fiancée. They were getting married in a few days.

Hang on. Was she seriously having second thoughts about marrying him? Would she rather have Kalahari?

Over his dead body!

Unable to stand still, he paced the mancave, navigating around the snooker table, feeling overheated.

Wasn't it bad enough that he'd put up with too much shit already these past months?

First had been Zawadi's abdication. Next, Queen Zulekha had implied Zik was unsuitable for the crown. Then Kalahari had arrived, and the king had announced him as his second son, born out-of-wedlock. Finally, Kalahari was challenging the succession and bidding for his right to inherit the crown.

All these within two months. Add in the pandemic and everything associated, and Zik's stress level was through the roof.

Extra responsibilities have been dumped on his shoulders, and at the same time, he'd been told he couldn't be king. On top of that, he couldn't hang out with his friends to unwind as usual. The only de-stresser he had was when he spent a few hours chatting with his friends and playing online games.

He missed the weekends where he would hang out with his brothers in the games room after rugby practice. They hadn't done that in six months because of the restrictions. Unlike his brothers who seemed to just get on with their lives, Zik struggled without the social contact.

So the only ray of sunshine in the past few months had been Amara accepting to marry him. Yes, their relationship wasn't ideal. Still, there'd been a rapport in their banter. And there'd been a hint of willingness to make it work for them.

Now, it all seemed up in the air again.

But he'd had enough. If Amara thought he would walk away from her, then she needed her head examined.

A woman providence had gifted him after more than a decade of living in misery. He would not give her up. Not now.

He grabbed his phone, scrolled through the contacts, and dialled the number he needed. It rang several times.

"Azikiwe, it's almost midnight. What's going on?" Kalahari said when the line connected.

"We need to talk." He didn't care how late it was or if he'd woken Kal from sleep.

"Can't it wait until morning?"

"No, it can't. I'm in the Games Room."

Kalahari sighed. "I'll be there in ten minutes."

The line disconnected, and Zik walked to the bar, grabbing the whiskey bottle. He pulled out two glasses and placed them on the granite counter. His fingertips tapped against the hard top as he waited.

The door swung open, and his brother walked in, wearing a dampened tank top and sweats with trainers. He looked like he'd just had a hard workout.

"Would you like a drink?" Zik raised the bottle.

"Not right now. Keep your enemies closer—is that your plan?" Kal stopped in the middle of the room and folded his hands in front of him. "You had something to say. So get to it."

Okay. Zik walked around the counter and stood in front of Kal, matching his pose.

"Look. I think it's awful that you haven't been part of this family for so long, and I'm glad you're a part of us now. If you want a chance at the crown, you are welcome to give it your best shot and best of luck to you. But you're going to have to do it without Amara."

"Amara?" Kal raised one brow.

"Yes, Amara Onoh." Zik narrowed his eyes. "I'm willing to go to war for her. I won't give her up again."

"Noted, but what's that got to do with me? I have no interest in Amara Onoh. If you want her, go get her."

"I intend to."

"Good." Kal glanced around the place. "So, this is the famous Games Room. What were you playing on the console?"

Zik jerked back. He hadn't been expecting this to be so easy. He scrubbed a palm over his beard. "Grand Theft Auto Online. Do you play?"

"Not computer games. But I'm up for some snooker if you are. Unless you were heading to bed."

"Sure. I'm up for it. Would you like that drink now?"

"Yes," Kal said as he grabbed a cue stick and set up the balls. "What's this about you giving up Amara?"

"I'll tell you mine if you tell me yours," Zik said.

"Touché." Kal chuckled.

CHAPTER EIGHT

September 2020, Nigeria

"You know I thought this was a prank at first. But you're actually doing it," said Joya, one of Amara's closest friends, as she handed a round powder brush to the makeup artist.

"I am." Excitement fluttered in Amara's belly. She sat on a stool while the stylist applied finishing touches to her makeup. Her wedding day had landed.

She used one of the spare bedrooms in her family home to get ready because she didn't want strangers traipsing in and out of her private quarters during the wedding ceremony. She had a hair and makeup artist as well as personal stylist to dress her. Not to mention all the other people— extended relatives, catering team—associated with organising the event.

It had been a week since she and Zik had had an argument via text messaging and she'd blocked his number in anger. She'd thought he would try to appease her by posting an apology online. Instead, he hadn't posted anything on his social media accounts for over a week.

The only way she'd known he remained alive and intended to go through with the wedding had been through her brothers—Ekene who'd returned to their hometown two days ago and Ejike who came last night. Also, her mother was regularly on the phone with Queen Sapphire dealing with any last-minute hiccups.

Yesterday, she'd unblocked Zik's number to see if he'd sent any messages which hadn't come through or had tried to call her.

Nothing. Nada.

The jerk hadn't tried to contact her at all.

Yet, he was here today to wed her.

What kind of a human being was she marrying? How could their last communication be an argument, yet he would still show up here?

Not that she didn't want him. Far from it. She couldn't handle any more disappointments and rejections.

So yes, she was glad he'd kept to his end of the bargain.

However, was their stalemate a sign of their future together?

If the argument had been with Zawadi—not that she'd had many of those with her ex—the man would try to appease her to resolve the matter.

But Zik wasn't even budging. Another reason why they were not compatible. How could he not even try to appease her a little?

Couldn't he see she'd been worried about him enough to text him after the phone call she'd had with Ekene that night?

"I noticed. You look amazing," Joya commented, reclaiming Amara's attention. Her patterned burnt orange and black mouth covering matched the square-neck, fitted-bodice long dress. She'd arrived yesterday with Ejike as they lived in Abuja, separately. But it made sense for them to travel together to the wedding.

For the ceremony, they'd had to limit the number of attendees due to government restrictions. To make up for the lack of party crowds, the palace had sent out five-kilo bags of rice, portions of meat from the slaughtered cows, bottles of drinks, and other cooking condiments to each household in the clan so they could cook and eat at home because they couldn't be at the party. They'd also been sent other commemorative souvenirs with Amara's and Zik's photos printed on them.

"It's such a shame there won't be many young men to choose from, now that you've taken Zik off the market," Uchenna, her cousin who sat on the bed, said.

Amara's spine stiffened at the way her cousin had casually mentioned Zik's name. She narrowed her eyes. Uchenna's tone meant something nasty was about to go down, and Amara would not bare her privacy to the public.

She turned to the makeup artist. "Please excuse us."

"Yes, Your Highness." The woman packed up her things, left the room, and shut the door.

"What's going on?" Joya asked, folding her arms.

Amara raised her hand, swivelled, and faced her cousin who stared boldly at her. "Uchenna, how do you know my husband?"

"Your husband, kwa. Have you married him already?" The woman had the audacity to answer snidely.

"Bia, Uchenna. Akpasukwana m iwe. Don't get me angry," she warned, suddenly on the verge of fury.

Sure, her cousin was correct. She wasn't yet married to Zik. At best, he would be her fiancé until all the rites were completed. Still, somehow, she'd felt territorial about him from the moment he'd proposed to her. And the way this one casually mentioned him raised her suspicions.

"Hian. What did I do wrong?" Her cousin tried to look innocent, flicking her acrylic nails.

Joya's gaze bounced between them. "Amara, calm down."

"Tell her to answer the question. How does she know Zik?" Amara didn't always get along with her cousin, yet restrictions meant she couldn't have her full bridal entourage. Uchenna was her first cousin, and her parents were here. It made sense for her to be involved in getting Amara ready.

"How else does a woman know a man?" Uchenna said in an amused tone.

"What the hell. You slept with him! How could you?"

"Look who's talking. Were you not engaged to his brother? How was I to know you would switch over to this one?"

"Get out of my room. Get out!" Cold fury iced Amara's veins. She'd known Zik had had many lovers. But she'd never contemplated she would encounter one of his conquests in her family. This was just too much.

"You heard her," Joya said to Uchenna.

"I'm going," her cousin grumbled before leaving.

"I can't do this. I can't do this." Amara stood, yanked the hem of her long marigold lace and silk dress, and paced.

"Yes, you can." Joya tried to appease her. "You can't let her spoil your day."

"Didn't you hear her? How many more of his exes am I going to encounter? I mean, I knew what he was. I always had my doubts about marrying him. And this is exactly the reason."

Joya blocked her path and placed her hands on Amara's shoulders.

"You said it yourself. You knew what he was. Yet, he is forsaking all others for you. He came here for you. Uchenna is jealous because you did what she couldn't. You bagged him. He is yours now. Everyone else is an ex. Done. Finito. Over."

Amara puffed out a heavy breath. "You're right. The heifer was trying it. But she's toast."

"Damn right she is."

They both giggled.

"Keep her out of my way for the rest of the day."

"On it."

"Thank you." She had half a mind to tell the guards to walk Uchenna out. But her parents were here as part of the Umunna who would perform the marriage rites. And she didn't want any disruptions to the day if she had to explain why she was kicking her cousin out.

"Amara." Someone tapped on the door.

"I'll get it," Joya said and pulled the panel. "Isha!"

"Joya." The two of them did a side embrace before Zik's sister stepped into the room. She was dressed in similar colours as Joya, burnt orange and black, to signify she was a friend of the bride, but her long-sleeved, A-line maxi dress had a mulberry-coloured sash around the empire line. The mulberry was the Saene family colour. "Wow. Amara, you are stunning. My brother won't know what hit him."

"You think?" Warmth spread through Amara.

"I know. They sent me to come and get you. Your husband is waiting." Isha beamed a smile.

For the first time, it hit her. She was about to wed Zik. How did she get here? What was she doing? She held her breath, trying to contain her sudden panic. Two months ago, she hated him. She still wasn't enthralled with him—the incident with Uchenna was a prime example. She shouldn't have accepted Zik's proposal.

But no one was forcing her to do this, just circumstances.

Two months ago, she'd been preparing to marry his brother. Then Zawadi had humiliated her by rejecting her. Although she was still uncertain about Zik, she couldn't back out of this marriage. Couldn't live with the disgrace. Couldn't give up on the years of preparation, of being groomed to be the future queen of Bagumi. After all, she was Africa's most celebrated princess. This was the life she'd been raised to expect. She had to stay calm.

Cool, calm, collected. Some people had named her the ice princess, after all. And she was dressed like one, draped in a couture gown worth thousands of dollars—the first of three outfits for the day—and jewellery, not to mention the costs of retaining the stylists for the day or the spa treatments she'd undertaken.

She followed the women downstairs. Joya held the train of her dress to keep her from tripping.

Music blasted from the speakers, the DJ already set up under one of the canopies. There would be a live band later in the day for the actual wedding reception.

They had to get through other rituals first. Like getting the consent of her Umunna, the extended family, for the wedding and then Zik's family paying the dowry.

The spacious gazebo had been decorated festively with flowers and crystal decorations, making it look like a glittering wonderland. A long red carpet stretched across the courtyard from the door.

Seated on settees on one side was her family— her father, His Majesty Igwe Obiora Ernest Onoh, her mother Queen Ego, oldest brother Osita, her uncle and aunt. On the other side were King

Ibrahim, Queen Sapphire, Zik, and his brother Zediah.

"Adaeze, bia. Come," Uchenna's father beckoned.

Adaeze literally meant daughter of the king and was how many people in her hometown addressed her.

Joya and Isha waited by the house while Amara walked the rest of the way on the plush carpet. Years of practice ensured she didn't snag her stilettoes on the hem of the silk gown embedded with thousands of crystals.

Her skin prickled, and she glanced in Zik's direction. Even seated, he looked imposing and regal dressed in the mulberry-mauve embroidered tunic and trouser set. He was usually dressed in European suits so it seemed like beholding him for the first time in this attire. She hadn't looked at him properly in a long time because she tended to avoid him. During Riona's baby shower about six months ago, she hadn't noticed much of him.

Zik was gorgeous, no doubt about it. Maybe because she hadn't seen him physically since they got engaged, he took her breath away. The short hair, dark eyes, slash of cheekbones, and sensuous lips. The most noticeable change since the last time she'd seen him? He'd grown a beard, trimmed neatly. He looked virile and powerful. Grown.

He watched her with an intensity she'd never known, and she had to break the gaze so she wouldn't stumble as her knees wobbled.

She kept her stare fixed at her father when she reached the bottom of the gazebo, gathered the hem of her skirt, and sank into a deep graceful curtsy. "Your Majesties, Your Graces."

"Rise, our daughter," her uncle said. "Do you know this young man here, Azikiwe?"

This was part of the formal process for her clan to conduct the marriage ritual. Although the proposal had already been made and accepted, it had to be done again in front of her people.

Amara met Zik's unwavering gaze. Butterflies fluttered in her belly, and her cheeks heated. "Yes, Uncle. I know him."

"Good. Azikiwe came with his family and brought many gifts. He says he wants to marry you. Do you want to marry him? Should we accept his gifts?"

She met Zik's gaze again. His expression left her breathless. They were not married yet. If she turned him down now, it would all be over. Yet, his gaze said he'd claimed her already. That she was his. That he knew she would say yes.

Her mouth dried out, and her heart raced. Movement at the edge of her vision made her glance there. Uchenna stood at the edge of the gazebo, arms crossed over her chest, watching.

Amara's jaw tightened, and she fought to maintain her composure.

To hell with this. She was going to say yes. She was going to become Zik's wife. But he was still an arrogant jerk. And if he thought he would get an easy ride with her, he had another think coming.

"Yes, Uncle. Accept his gifts. I will marry him."

CHAPTER NINE

Zik was married. Finally.

The thought played in his mind as he sat in the royal executive vehicle with the emblems and flag, travelling from Darusa airport. The rest of his family were in different vehicles heading back to the palace.

Amara sat at the other end of the backseat, her gaze fixed out the window although he doubted she could see clearly through the tinted glass given the encroaching darkness outside.

This was the first time they'd been alone all day, and today was the first time he'd seen her physically since she'd attended his sister-in-law's baby shower earlier in the year.

Interesting that when he'd had to choose one of his brothers to attend the wedding, due to restrictions on number of guests, he'd chosen Zediah. For starters, he'd been the least problematic. Zawadi was out of the question after what he'd done to Amara. Zik couldn't have subjected Amara to seeing him so soon, especially on her wedding day.

Kalahari had been the second least because although he and Zik had cleared the air with regards to Amara, Zik couldn't trust him to have his back one hundred percent.

That had left the twins. Zediah had been an easy pick because he was the closest to Zik in temperament, adaptable and sensitive. In contrast, Zareb was too rigid and oblivious. Also, Zed could read him without verbal cues, a habit they'd learned when they used to play music together as children. This would've proven helpful today had he needed his brother's support more deeply.

Now, he stared at Amara. He'd seen her in three outfits today, and each time, she'd looked stunning and sparkling. Right now, she wore an embroidered mulberry fitted-bodice dress with crystals around the hems. She'd started off the day in the Onoh colours of marigold and ended up in the purple colours of the Saenes, signifying she was now one of them.

He loved the symbolism.

She was now a part of his family. A part of him.

Nothing else made him happier.

However, she didn't seem super-pleased to be with him. She'd barely said two words to him through the day.

He understood it had been a few hectic weeks and today would be overwhelming with all the activities.

Images from the wine-carrying played in his mind.

Amara had danced around the wedding reception venue to the music of the live band, searching for him among the guests. On finding him, she'd knelt before him, handed over the glass of palm wine, and her gaze had lowered shyly.

He'd glimpsed a different side of her, not the abrasive online persona she projected. Hyper-aware and pulse racing, he'd never been more enchanted by her.

Because in that moment, it'd felt like she truly wanted him, rather than what he represented—the throne of Bagumi. And he knew that once he drank from the glass, she would become officially his wife. He'd drunk the wine, stuffed some naira notes into the empty glass, then he'd leaned forward, kissed the corner of her lips, and whispered, "Thank you, babygirl."

The crowd had cheered and applauded. Amara had met his gaze, but the shutters from earlier in the day seemed to have returned. They'd gotten through the rest of the event barely talking, although they'd smiled for the cameras and done everything else as a couple.

"Where are we going?"

Her sharp voice cut through his thoughts.

He glanced at her. In the dark car, her expression was shadowed.

"You're finally talking to me," he said, grabbing a bottle of water from the freezer compartment.

"I don't know what you're talking about." She turned away from him again.

He poured water into a glass. "Here, have a drink."

She shifted, glanced from him to the glass in his hand. "You're offering me water. Why?"

"Because I didn't see you eat or drink during the reception." He held out the glass, concerned she would be dehydrated from the day's heat and activities. He knew how stressful the day had been, and it couldn't have been any easier for her. "I know because I was too anxious to eat, too. It's not every day you get married."

Her mouth dropped open as she gasped. Was she shocked he would admit to anxiety? Perhaps she'd been expecting some machismo from him. For him to pretend he'd been perfectly cool with everything.

Her shoulder rose and fell, and she took the glass, taking a long sip. "I wasn't hungry."

"One," he said and took another glass.

"One what?" she asked.

He poured the water, took a deep drink before replying. "I'm counting each time you're rude."

He usually bent over backwards to make other people happy. However, he expected basic courtesy from everyone including his bride. Plus, his bullshit meter had become extra touchy recently.

"How was I rude?" she snapped.

"I offered you a drink, and you didn't say thank you when you accepted it. Even if you didn't want it, the correct response should be 'no, thanks.' Being polite doesn't cost you anything."

"Thank you," she grumbled and looked away.

Silence descended for several minutes. He settled for observing the gentle rise and fall of her chest as he waited for her to say something else.

"You still haven't told me where we're going. It doesn't take this long to get to Darusa Palace," she said finally.

"We're not going to DP," he said. "We'll be spending the next week at Beya Castle."

"Beya Castle?" Her face rumpled. "Isn't that place old and dilapidated? Why are we going there?"

He chuckled. He could imagine the old castle built in the 1500s would not be a place a modern princess would like to visit.

"Because it's my ancestral home and my country home. Plus, it has a dungeon where I can lock up my unruly wife if she gives me too much of a headache."

"You're not serious." Her eyes bulged as she jerked backwards.

"Absolutely serious," he deadpanned.

"Yeah, whatever. I know you're just pulling my leg. It's the twenty-first century, and it's illegal to keep dungeons."

"If you say so."

"Seriously. Tell me where we're going."

"Tell me why you blocked my number."

"Because you were being a jerk."

"How was I being a jerk when you were talking about marrying my brother?"

"Well, I married you, didn't I?" She glared at him.

"Yes, you did." He puffed out heavy breath. This was a good time as any to settle this issue. "And I want to leave everything that came before behind us. I know we're both here out of obligation to our families, but surely, you feel something for me."

She snorted in derision. "Feel something for you? Look, I don't even like you!"

That felt like a blow to his gut, and he jerked back.

"What have I done to you to deserve this hatred?"

He understood her anger, considering the circumstances. However, he was the good guy here. His mother had begged him to save Amara from humiliation, and he'd done the decent thing.

Still, the level of vitriol in her tone indicated there was more going on.

"You're not Zawadi," she bit out in a contempt-filled voice, her gaze fixed at a point beyond his right shoulder, her chin tilted imperiously.

Talk about a body-slam. That fucking hurt. He hated being compared to his older brother. He'd done everything not to be like the 'perfect' Zawadi. However, it seemed he'd fallen way short of Amara's standards.

"And yet, he jilted you." As soon as he said it, he regretted it. She was hitting below the belt. Didn't mean he had to hit back.

Her eyes widened and then narrowed. The haughty expression returned to her face as she straightened her shoulders. "And this shows how low I've fallen when I end up with a jerk like you."

"Excuse you." Zik leaned towards her. "Zawadi jilts you, and *I'm* the jerk? Just in case it skipped your mind, I saved your face out there. I stepped in and rescued you and your family from the public humiliation."

The palace press coordinator had spun the story in the media—Zik and Amara had always been in love. Zawadi's abdication only provided an opening for them to be together.

"Exactly." She glared at him and yanked her arm back when he reached for her. "It is your brother's mess, and you're the one cleaning it up. So, you will put up with my scorn and hatred for however long I deem it reasonable."

He lowered his head, shaking it. He was trying to understand her motivations, but she was not making it easy. "Where do you get off comparing me to Zawadi and holding me for his faults?"

"Because Zawadi didn't have sex with my cousin!" she gritted out in a low voice as if suddenly conscious there were other people in the car although the privacy screen separated them from the driver and security personnel in front.

His back stiffened, and he raised his head. "Your cousin? Who the fuck is that?"

"Uchenna Onoh. She was at the ceremony today," she spat out angrily.

"And so? Am I harassing you about your sex life? About sleeping with my brother? No. What happened in the past is in the past. I'm not going to justify my sex life to you or anyone else. I promised to be faithful to you, and that should be enough for you."

"No, it's not. Not when your exes show up at my wedding. Not when they are members of my family. No, your promise is not enough." Her voice was cold, dripping with contempt.

"Then we're at an impasse because this is not going to work. I'm not going to live with a woman who hates me. With a woman who can't see anything good in me." He scrubbed a hand over his face.

Should he go on here? All things considered, maybe he should. His patience was running thin right now. He didn't have it in him to play the diplomat walking on eggshells.

"I know you hold Zawadi as the ideal husband and ideal king. But I'll tell you one thing. I love Bagumi as much as he does. You will find no one who loves this country more than I do. If I become king, I'll become Bagumi, and Bagumi will become me. So since you've made it quite clear that you cannot love me, I will assume you cannot love Bagumi. Therefore, when our trial period ends, I'll release you from the marriage contract, and you can return home free from any obligations to me or Bagumi."

"What?" She flicked the light switch, and a white glow illuminated her shocked expression.

He met her gaze, held it so she would see how serious he was. "I will not subject the people of this country to a queen who holds them in contempt."

"I don't hold them in contempt." She appeared appalled at his suggestion.

He tilted his head. "Don't you?"

"You're implying because I dislike you that means I dislike Bagumi."

"If I become king, Bagumi and I will become one and the same. Everything good about it will be me, and everything bad about it will be me. There is no separation. That's what it means to be an absolute monarch."

He would take on the role of king if deemed worthy, but he didn't hunger for it as much as she seemed to hunger to be queen. That was the only reason she'd married him. Not because she wanted to build a future with him. All she wanted was the status that came with the throne.

"You're not king yet," her voice trembled.

He could almost hear the wheels spinning in her mind. Would she call his bluff?

"Exactly. Without you around, I don't need to be king. I can hand it all over to Zediah. Riona would probably be a more loving queen, anyway," he threw in.

They'd see how Amara liked being compared to others, since she was quick to contrast him to Zawadi.

"You're serious." Her back stiffened, her eyes glaring.

"I am. You leave me with little choice. As I said, I will not subject this country to a queen who doesn't deserve their loyalty and adulation."

She didn't reply for several seconds. The car pulled to a stop, and the doors opened. He turned to get out.

"Wait," she said. "Are you threatening me? Are you saying I must love you or go home?"

"You could see it that way." He shrugged in resignation, knowing the ball was in her court. "Or you could give us a chance to become the best that we can be together. Your choice, babygirl."

He would not beg for what was his already. He turned and stepped out into the warm night, knowing the weeks ahead would be difficult.

CHAPTER TEN

What the hell? How could Zik threaten to send her home after the trial? He'd just threatened to end their marriage after a month.

Amara took a few seconds to compose herself after Zik left before she swung her feet out of the car.

He stood outside the door in his regal glory and extended his hand to help her out.

Huffing, she ignored him, gathered her long skirt so she didn't trip, and straightened. She didn't need his help for anything. If he was going to give her ultimatums, he would soon learn that she didn't cower easily. She wasn't some naïve girl he'd just married from the village.

To think that he hadn't even tried to apologise for one of his conquests being at their wedding. Sure, he couldn't have helped Uchenna's presence. Still, it was his fault. If he hadn't slept with her cousin, there wouldn't be a problem. She wouldn't have had to deal with the woman's attitude today.

So what if he wasn't asking about her sex life. She didn't have numerous exes, and Zawadi hadn't been at the wedding. Hence he didn't have that reminder on their big day.

Anyway, she would call his bluff on the ultimatum. He would not send her home just because she didn't love him. No way was he going to give up on being the future king. No one in their right mind would give up on being the king of a country, certainly not someone raised as a prince.

The steady rhythmic sounds of drums drew her attention to the small crowd outside the impressive three-level mansion built in the quadrangular style of ancient Bagumian homes crossed with a medieval castle.

Maybe because it was dark and lit by floodlights, the amazing new structure looked different from the old one she'd seen many years ago as a child when she'd first explored the place on a historical tour of Bagumi. The one she remembered had been one of the gatehouses to the fortress castle carved in the mountain famed to have sheltered citizens from the transatlantic slave trade and colonial invasion.

"Welcome home, Onyi and Onyia of Beya," someone announced, and the crowd of about twenty people including the drummers prostrated.

From her history lessons, Onyi and Onyia were titles equivalent to Duke and Duchess, making them the Duke and Duchess of Beya. She hadn't been expecting this and hadn't been aware that Zik held any other titles outside of Prince.

Then again, he could have been gifted a duchy by his father as a wedding present or because he was the Interim Crown Prince until a decision was made on the succession.

"Thank you. I'm pleased to see you all," she said aloud and then lowered her voice for Zik's ears only. "I didn't know you organised a welcome party."

"I didn't organise it. They did," he said in an equally low tone and then raised his voice to say, "Rise. Thank you for welcoming my wife so warmly. Amara, these are the castle employees."

And then, he was introducing her to the staff, one-by-one. Of course, she couldn't remember everyone's name by the time he was done. He then guided her up the front steps.

Somebody released confetti, and it streamed down around her. Except this wasn't paper, but pink and white and orange scented flower petals, drifting over her head and shoulders. People cheered and clapped. She caught bits of French, English, and a language she assumed was Beya.

For a brief moment, it appeared to be a fantasy world and she expected Zik to sweep her off her feet and carry her across the threshold. Still angry with him, she wouldn't allow him to touch her.

In any case, he walked ahead, ignoring her.

Okay. Maybe he wasn't into such gestures as they were 'western' rather than 'African.'

Tilting her chin up, she entered the brightly lit marbled foyer where a crystal chandelier dangled from the high ceiling. A double staircase led to the next level while an archway stood between the stairs, leading into a wide corridor.

"You're probably tired." Zik turned to her. "I would recommend getting an early night and doing the tour of the castle tomorrow. What would you rather do?"

For the first time since they'd left Nigeria, she took a proper look at him in the light. How was he doing this? How did he know she was exhausted? It was like he was reading her, studying her. Observing her.

He'd done it in the car when he'd offered her water and said he'd noticed she hadn't eaten during the ceremony. Zawadi had never noticed such things about her. If she wasn't vocal about something, he wouldn't pay attention.

Yet, Zik had observed her during the wedding and had spotted she hadn't eaten. Had made the effort to ensure she wasn't dehydrated.

Perhaps now, he saw the fatigue in her eyes and the strain around her shoulders.

She had to give this to him, regardless of all his other faults. He paid attention to her. More than his brother ever did.

Her legs weakened, and she felt light-headed. She rubbed a palm over her face.

"Are you okay?" He reached out.

She jerked away. She might be exhausted, but she was not giving in to him. He had to take back his threat before he could touch her. "Just show me to the bedroom."

His jaw tightened, and he puffed out a heavy breath. "This way."

She followed him up two flights of stairs to the top level.

"This entire floor is our private quarters." He pushed open a door to a large bedroom with cream walls and pastel beddings and a settee. A replica of her bedroom at home.

Warmth flooded her body, and a huge smile covered her face, her tiredness forgotten. "Wow. How did you know?"

She glanced at him, already taking her shoes off so she could sink her feet into the silver shaggy rug at the foot of the bed.

"I asked Ekene, and he helped me pick out some of the things you like." He leaned against the door, hands shoved into his trouser pockets.

"It's wonderful. Thank you." She sank her bare feet into the plush rug and sighed as the sensation soothed her sore feet.

"You're welcome." He didn't budge from the spot.

She sat on the settee at the foot of the bed and watched him as silence hung over them, intimate and expectant. This was her husband, and he was gorgeous, just leaning there against the post, hands in his pockets in a casual manner. His tunic couldn't hide the width of his shoulders, nor the depth of his muscular chest. He might be a prince, but he had the body of an athlete acquired from training for the princes' rugby squad.

Her pulse quickened. She could understand why women fell over themselves to be near him, to be photographed with him. She grew warm, and her cheeks burned, just thinking about how it would feel to have him in bed with her. In bed … hang on.

"I'm assuming this is my room," she asked tentatively, realising the space was way too feminine for him.

"Yes, it is."

His deep voice sounded smooth and seductive all of a sudden. His mouth made her think of kissing and sex. His gaze met hers, and her heart jolted, her chest squeezing tight in protest. Like a thunderbolt, hot and electric, her knees buckled, and she was glad to be sitting already.

"Do you sleep here as well?" she asked, in a croaky voice, heat burning her cheeks. Why was she even embarrassed to ask the question? He was her husband.

"No. My room is next door. That's the interconnecting door." He pointed at the white slab in the middle of the cream wall. "The other one is your bathroom. I have one attached to mine, too. You can also find a walk-in wardrobe for your clothes back there. The lounge is across the hall." He pointed over his shoulder. "I have an office on this floor as well. And there is a small kitchen, too. But the main castle kitchen is downstairs. Due to the pandemic, I limit who comes up here. The staff won't come unless summoned, and the cleaning team show up every other day, unless you want them daily."

"No. That's fine."

"Good. I'm sure you'll figure the rest out as we go. There are phone numbers on the notepad on your bedside, in case you need to make emergency calls or summon the staff. There's also a bell by the wall. Your clothes should be stowed away already. I'm going to request for dinner to be brought up in thirty minutes. Does that give you enough time to shower and change?"

That was a lot of information to absorb. But she nodded. "Sure. It works."

"Good. Just walk through to the next room if you need anything else."

He strode out, shutting the door behind him.

Amara slumped on the settee. Things hadn't gone exactly as planned.

Zik seemed to have arranged for them to live separate lives anyway by giving her a different bedroom. And by his actions this evening, he didn't seem keen for physical contact with her. It was their wedding night. Wasn't he going to touch her? Kiss her? Make love to her?

Didn't all men want those things on their wedding night?

Maybe after she showered, she could change into one of those sexy lingerie her friends had gifted her. Between Isha and Joya, she had quite a selection designed to drive Zik insane with desire.

The goal for tonight would be to make him see what he would miss if he sent her home. After all, this was Zik, a man who loved sex, according to his reputation. He supposedly couldn't resist women, right? And she was a woman.

Undressing quickly, she entered the bathroom, covered her hair with a shower cap, and washed under the spray with gel and loofah. Her body had already been scrubbed and waxed and plucked at the spa yesterday. When she came out of the shower, she dried it and massaged oil over her skin. Then she dressed in a black baby-doll set barely covering her bum and showing off her décolletage, a short black silk robe over it.

Afterwards, she walked out of the room on bare feet, the marble floor cool underneath.

Zik sat in the living room, TV flickering. He stood. "There you are. Dinner is on the table. Enjoy the meal."

He headed past her towards the door.

"Aren't you eating, too?" she asked, confused.

"I ate a little. But I'm exhausted. I haven't slept in about a week, so I need to get to bed. But stay, enjoy the meal, watch TV if you want. I'll see you in the morning. Good night."

He left without giving her a second glance.

Amara stood there with her mouth open, flabbergasted. Zik hadn't even checked out her attire. She'd gone to all the trouble for nothing, since he wouldn't even look at her. She flopped onto the sofa, head in her hands.

What was really going on here?

CHAPTER ELEVEN

Zik strode along the corridor towards the living room, fixing his cufflinks. A glance at his gold wristwatch showed it was a quarter to ten o'clock in the morning. He had a briefing with his assistant at ten.

He wasn't usually up this late. But he hadn't slept as well as he'd wanted.

Mainly because Amara hadn't slept well, either.

After he'd left her in the living room, he'd returned to his bedroom and climbed into bed. Sleep hadn't come for a long time.

First, Amara had done a lot of pacing and muttering to herself. Then there'd been the sound of the TV into the early hours of the morning. When he'd eventually slept it, had been around four a.m., from sheer exhaustion.

He'd left his bedroom door slightly open so he could listen out in case Amara needed him. It was her first night in this house so he'd been worried about how she would settle in. That was the reason he'd gone through the effort of making sure the interior decorator connected with Ekene to get the details of her bedroom in Nigeria.

He'd wanted her to feel at home. Packing up and moving to another country couldn't be easy, even if she'd been preparing for it through her adult life. Still, she'd left her comfort zone, and he'd wanted her to have a relief area here, too, hence the bedroom just for her.

To be fair, the idea hadn't been entirely his. At first, he'd wanted her moving into his bedroom and using the one she currently had as her office or closet.

Then Isha had suggested a trial period to help ease him and Amara into the marriage so they could 'date' like normal individuals getting to know each other. She'd implied that people dating had the safety net of going back to their homes after hanging out with their partners. He'd realised Amara wouldn't have a safe space she could escape to if they shared a bedroom.

And having separate bedrooms seemed a great idea because he'd certainly not anticipated they would have a bitter confrontation on their wedding night. Also that the marriage would seem over before it had even started.

Sighing, he strolled into the living room, turned the corner, and halted. His heart slammed into his chest.

Amara lay in the corner of the sofa, asleep. Not actually lying, more like tucked into the corner, head on the armrest, feet curled under. The black silk robe covered her back and arms, not much else, the curve of her ebony thighs, the swell of her breasts, the hint of black lace thong between her ass cheeks all visible to him.

His body flooded with warmth, and his dick hardened, his heartbeat a steady drumbeat in his ears. Hell, he wanted his wife, in all the ways possible for him to have her. He'd been aching for her for so long, it had become a part of his existence.

But until this fracture between them was healed, they couldn't go there. He couldn't risk getting her pregnant and being lumbered with a wife who resented him because he'd forced her into a loveless marriage. He'd realised last night that as much as he desired her, he wanted her love more than he wanted her body or the throne. Hence, the impasse.

And the reason he'd walked out in such a hurry last night when she'd entered the living room dressed in the short robe and sexy lingerie. That one look at her and he'd been a goner. No way would he have stayed in there with her without eating her instead of the food. Escaping the tempting sight of her had been the only viable option.

But damn, she was beautiful and petite when she slept. His first impulse was to carry her into the bedroom so she could be comfortable. She must have fallen asleep much later than him. He took a step towards her and halted, curling his hands into fists by his sides.

He couldn't touch her. She'd made it abundantly clear last night he wasn't permitted to touch her. In the car, she'd jerked away when he'd tried to hold her hand during their argument. Later, when he stood outside the car and had tried to help her out, she'd ignored his outstretched hands. The final cue had been when she'd looked dizzy and he'd reached out to stop her from falling, and she'd backed away from him.

He wasn't entirely sure if this was because of their confrontation or if she didn't like body contact. He understood the implications of non-consensual contact. So until she gave him explicit permission to touch her, he would not try it again.

But he couldn't leave her here, exposed like this. His assistant would arrive shortly, and other staff members could pop in accidentally. No way would he allow anyone see her this exposed.

He hurried into his room, grabbed the purple velvet blanket from the foot of the bed, returned to the living room, and spread it over her.

She stirred, mumbled something, but didn't wake.

He took one last look at the petite bundle, resisting the urge to press his lips to her temple. He stepped back, walked out, and gently shut the door.

Deciding to give Amara the chance to sleep, Zik hurried to the top floor office, grabbed his laptop and phone, and descended to the ground floor wing which housed the official offices.

"Good morning, Your Royal Highness." Lucas bowed as Zik entered the foyer. "*Je suis désolé. Je n'savais pas que j'étais en retard. Je vous apportais juste votre café.*"

"No need to apologise, Lucas." Zik smiled reassuringly. His assistant always reverted to French whenever he was distressed. "You're not late. I decided to come downstairs instead. My wife is tired and still sleeping. I didn't want her disturbed."

"Oh. Of course, Onyi." The man swallowed and dipped his chin, blushing. "We can have this meeting much later, so you can get some sleep, too."

Zik chuckled at the man's embarrassment. His assistant probably thought Amara was still asleep because Zik had kept her awake doing pleasurable wedding night activities. If only the man knew.

"It's fine, Lucas. Just bring me the coffee, and we can get started with the items on the agenda."

He strode into his office. He'd gone for a modern glass and steel look with plum leather and rugs when he'd refurbished and redecorated the old castle. The various shades of purple, reflecting the Saene family colours and emblem, ran through the whole place.

"Yes, sir." Lucas popped out while Zik set up his laptop.

The young man returned with a silver tray laden with a flask, porcelain mugs, and a bowl with brown sugar cubes. He placed it on the glass table and poured black coffee from the flask into a mug, which he then placed on the metal coaster which had the Royal House of Saene emblem.

"How is your mother?" Zik asked like he did at the start of every week.

Lucas was a Beya local much like everyone else working directly for him. His mother, Mrs Bene, was the principal of the high school not far from here. He'd started working for Zik straight after graduating from university last year. Zik had been involved in recruiting him as he'd been part of Zik's Youth Leadership scheme which sponsored young, bright Bagumian talent.

When he became Interim Crown Prince, the head of palace staff had suggested reassigning Lucas and giving Zik an older staff more used to the office of the crown prince. Zik had refused. Most of the staff in the crown prince office were rigid and strict on protocols. All about the old guard and hierarchy, regardless of talent or personality. He trusted Lucas because the young man understood him.

"My mother is well, sir," Lucas replied.

"And the school. I hope she has everything they require for the start of the new academic year."

Lucas frowned. "Well, she has an issue with available teachers because some have not returned. She's afraid she might have to send some students home in the meantime."

Zik leaned back into his chair. "Oh. I didn't know. I would like to help if I can. Remind me to speak to her as soon as we finish here."

"Okay, sir. I'll make a note." Lucas typed onto his tablet device.

Zik scrolled through his emails checking for anything marked urgent and found none. He was newly married and had a week off official duties, so there shouldn't be any pressing issues coming his way.

However, there were still emails that needed his attention. And he would rather be down here working than upstairs pining for his wife who hated him.

He sipped his coffee as he discussed any issues with Lucas and rattled out instructions.

"One last item, sir," Lucas said. "Now that the official account has been set up for the Onyi and Onyia of Beya, DP wants to close down the personal social media profiles for you and the Onyia by Monday next week."

Zik scratched his chin. He'd seen the email which had arrived sometime over the weekend but hadn't really paid it much attention. This was another way that DP tried to control his life now. They didn't want him acting on a personal capacity, claiming that his actions would reflect on the office of the crown prince.

While he accepted the logic to a certain degree, the social media account was a space for him to be more human with the citizens rather than them just reading official statements all the time.

Plus, he knew Amara would throw a fit when she found out the restrictions about to rain down on her social media. She would no longer be able to subtweet him.

He smiled, remembering their online banter. He would miss it if it disappeared.

"I'll have to discuss it with my wife and let you know what we decide," he said. "Was there anything else?"

"Just that you wanted to call my mother," Lucas replied.

"Good. Let me do it right away." Zik reached for his phone.

CHAPTER TWELVE

Amara woke to the feeling of being surrounded in a smoky, woody comforting scent reminding her of Zik's seductive and intoxicating spicy cardamon and rosewood cologne. It took her a few minutes to fully come awake and realise she lay on a deep velvet sofa in a living room with lilac walls, covered in a blanket against soft cushions rather than in bed beside Zik on their wedding night.

Light from the partly opened drapes indicated it was day, and the dark-wood door with an intricate design was closed. Sangria-hued throw cushions sat in cream-coloured 1950s style upholstered armchairs. The rug was a custom-made geo design matching the wall and provided a canvas for the rest of the furniture. Two recesses in the wall had built-in dark-wood shelves stacked with art pieces and books. With the green potted plants and vases with flowers, the soft textures and the vibrant colours, the space looked very romantic and stylish.

Not exactly the kind of layout she would have imagined a man to live in, let alone a prince. It showed an artistic, sensitive persona. Another pleasant surprise.

This was Zik's country home. Now her home, too.

Yesterday had been their marriage ceremony. The joy of celebrating with her family and friends seemed a long time ago because of her argument with Zik in the car last night. She hadn't expected him to give her an ultimatum or to even leave her alone on their wedding night.

But he'd left her right here in this living room while he'd gone to bed claiming he was tired. She'd gone through the effort of freshening up and dressing in sexy lingerie, all for nothing.

She'd thought he'd been bluffing, that he would come out later and apologise.

He hadn't.

She'd ended up watching TV because she couldn't sleep, and she must have fallen asleep on the sofa anyway.

So who'd covered her with the blanket? It had to be Zik. He'd come into this living room and found her on the sofa with skimpy clothing, and all he did was cover her up?

This was serious. Was he not attracted to her?

Her chest tightened as her body grew heavy. Zik the playboy didn't find her desirable? A ridiculous concept and yet hurtful to imagine.

She shoved the horrid feeling aside. She wouldn't give in to despair already, just one day into their married life. Getting off the sofa, she padded across the quiet hallway into her bedroom.

A trip to the bathroom afterwards and she completed her morning routine.

For her outfit, she chose a midi-length flared bronze dress with a pair of black roman sandals. Zik has said they would do a tour of the castle, and she needed to be comfortable and look informal.

Dressed, she walked through the corridors checking the other rooms. A den, a library, an office, a master bedroom and bathroom. All the doors were accessible except one. She wondered why that specific door was locked when Zik's bedroom was open.

In the kitchen, she found a bowl of fruits sitting on the granite counter and grabbed an apple. Famished, she opened the fridge and found a box of cupcakes. She didn't even think twice, grabbing a cake before going to pour some coffee from the coffeemaker. She didn't move from the kitchen until she'd finished two cupcakes and a mug of coffee.

Zik must have ordered the box of cupcakes for her. Since he'd gone to the effort of giving her a replica bedroom, it made sense he would order one of her favourite treats too. Her lips curled into a smile. He proved to be as considerate and generous as Isha had mentioned. Perhaps he wasn't as one-dimensional as she'd implied.

She returned to her bedroom and grabbed her phone, where she found a message from Zik.

Hope you slept well. I have to go out for a while. Lucas, my assistant, is available to attend to you and take you on the tour of the castle. I'll be back in time for dinner on the terrace at 6pm. See you later.

6pm? No. Where was Zik? This was their honeymoon. Their time together. He wasn't supposed to go anywhere without her. What was he playing at? She sent him a text.

Where are you?

Five minutes and no response from him.

Amara didn't like this at all. Adrenaline rushed through her, and she pressed her lips flat with suspicion.

Bad enough Zik had not touched her on their wedding night. Now, he was gone to who-knows-where. She couldn't just sit here all day waiting for him. She had to know where he was. She called the number for his assistant which was on the notepad on her bedside. It rang once before being answered.

"Good afternoon, Your Royal Highness," a young male voice said.

"Is this Lucas?" she asked. "Come up to the apartment."

"Yes, ma'am," he replied. "I'm on my way."

Less than five minutes later, a tap sounded on the door to the foyer. One of the guards standing outside pushed the panel open, and a twenty-something year-old man stepped in.

"Your Royal Highness, it's an honour to meet you." He bowed deep. He was stylishly dressed in a long-sleeved white dress shirt, navy embroidered waistcoat, and trousers.

Amara smiled at him. "It's nice to meet you, Lucas."

"Thank you, ma'am." He dipped again.

"You make me sound ancient when you call me ma'am," she said, trying to keep him sweet. She wasn't much older than him. If she was going to stay here, she had to make Zik's staff like her. She knew that much. There was no point forming hierarchy, especially when she needed allies. "You can call me Amara."

"No. I can't do that. You are the Onyia. I'll get fired." His eyes widened, and he appeared horrified.

"Okay. Why don't we try something different? Call me Mrs Zik."

"I don't know." His smile was tentative.

"It's fun and formal and you're not addressing me by my first name. Please?" She smiled in encouragement.

"Okay, ma," he said. She frowned, and he added. "Mrs Zik."

"That's better." She giggled, liking him already.

"Mrs Zik, should I ask the kitchen to bring some lunch for you?" he asked expectantly.

"That's not necessary. I ate some cupcakes already and drank coffee so I'm good for now."

"Cupcakes are not food, Mrs Zik." He smiled.

Amara patted his arm and walked into the living room. "Don't worry. Actually, Zik left a message to say he'd popped out, but I don't know where, and I'm all lonely here."

He followed her. "Oh, he's only gone to the school. He said I should show you around the castle."

Why would Zik be at a school? He'd promised he had no official engagements this week. He wasn't a teacher. Only parents would visit schools. Was he there because of a child?

She turned. "Oh, the school. Is that in Beya? I'd like to go there, too. Can you take me?"

"The prince wanted me to show you around the castle," Lucas said tentatively.

"The castle will still be here when we get back, and we can do the tour another day."

"Okay. Let me send him a message so he knows we're coming."

"No. Don't do that. I'd like to surprise him. You know, spontaneity and all that."

"Of course, Your Highness. Let me arrange the car and security."

Amara watched as he made a few phone calls, and ten minutes later, she was downstairs, out of the castle, and in the dark SUV on the way. Lucas sat in the backseat with her.

About twenty minutes later, the vehicle pulled into a large school premises. An archway announced Beya High School. Trees and hedges lined the streets leading to different blocks. The car stopped in front of an administrative building where the bodyguard opened the door, and Amara stepped out into the bright sunshine.

Lucas hurried to her side. "This way to the principal's office."

"Okay." She followed him.

Before they entered the building, a middle-aged woman in a dress suit came out. "Lucas, are you here to see His Royal Highness?"

"Yes, I'm his wife," Amara replied, a little miffed the woman didn't recognise her. But she supposed the face covering and her casual clothes made her appear ordinary.

"Pardon me, Your Royal Highness. We were not expecting you today." The woman curtsied. "Welcome to Beya High School. I'm Principal Bene."

"Nice to meet you, Principal. Please don't worry. I'm not here in an official capacity. If you can point us in the direction of where my husband is, Lucas can take me there."

"Of course, Onyia. He's in the Year 11 block. Lucas knows where it is."

"Thank you," Amara said and then turned to Lucas. "Lead the way."

She followed him with the bodyguard trailing behind.

"Lucas, how do you know the principal? Were you a student here?"

He dipped his head and nodded. "She's my mother."

"Your mum. Ah. No wonder she gave you that look like you should have warned her I was coming." She laughed.

The young man laughed, too. "She will tell me off tonight for not allowing her to prepare for your visit."

"If she does, I promise I'll make it up to you with cupcakes," she teased.

"Cupcakes is not food, Mrs Zik." He chuckled, glanced at the serious-looking bodyguard, and straightened. "This is the Year 11 block."

"Okay." They walked along the veranda of the light-yellow block, passing the doors and open windows for each class with a teacher standing in front of a blackboard and masked students sitting in rows and columns of two at desks.

Then she caught a glimpse of Zik, and her heart skipped a beat. She halted and raised her finger to her mask, indicating for Lucas and the bodyguard to be silent. Then she moved closer to the window so she could see properly.

Zik stood in front of a class of what looked like fifteen-to-sixteen-year-old boys and girls, the sleeves of his white shirt rolled up to his elbows, his jacket hanging over the back of a seat behind a desk. He would talk to the class, then scribble on the blackboard with a white chalk.

Amara stood there, skin tingling, heartbeat racing, mouth open, thankful for the face covering because it took several seconds before she could recover from the wonder of watching Zik teach.

Prince Azikiwe Saene. Player Zik. Playboy Extraordinaire ... was in a classroom teaching in a local school.

If she hadn't seen it with her own eyes, no one would have convinced her that it had happened. In fact, no one who knew him would ever believe it.

So she raised her phone, tapped the camera app, and started recording.

But after a while, she forgot she was recording, mesmerised by the way Zik owned the class. He was joking and laughing even as he was teaching the subject. The students were attentive, asking and answering questions.

This was a different Zik from the one she knew. The one photographed almost every month with a different woman. The one who loved to party.

This Zik was serious, grown, engaging young minds, imparting knowledge in his personal time. Of course, the school wasn't paying him for this. This Zik was giving back to the community. And even if he only taught for one day, these kids would never forget this experience.

He looked totally at ease. Like he'd done this before. It was obvious how much of a people's person he was. How much he loved engaging and interacting with people.

This was the kind of king the people needed. One who engaged with people on their level. Not one sitting in a tower giving out orders.

The class loved this Zik.

The people of Bagumi would love this Zik.

She could love this Zik.

The ringing bell jarred her from her thoughts, and she jerked away from the window.

"We have to go." She hurried back towards the car, suddenly afraid Zik would come out of the class and see her.

"Don't you want to see the Onyi?" Lucas asked, looking confused.

She couldn't blame him. She was confused, too. "I'll see him when he returns to the castle."

Thankfully, they managed to get back into the car and out of the school without being intercepted.

But her mind raced in different directions.

What had happened back there? Why did Zik not tell her where he was going? And why was she so enraptured by his presence in front of that classroom?

Even now, her heart was still thumping so fast and she was breathless with the adrenaline rush, her skin warm.

For a moment while standing outside that window, she'd felt something other than disdain for Zik—a warm, tingly feeling of euphoria and wonder. She'd felt energised and stimulated.

She'd wanted Zik, there and then. Even now, her nipples were stiff, her knickers dampened from arousal.

But how could she give herself to a man who would threaten to send her home because she didn't behave exactly the way he wanted?

She clenched her hands, nails biting into her palms as she fought not to growl in frustration.

CHAPTER THIRTEEN

Zik dropped his cutlery on the half-empty plate, averting his gaze from Amara who stabbed the food with her fork but didn't seem to have eaten much, either. He lowered his hands to his lap and stared at the distance.

They sat opposite each other, the table between them, on the castle roof terrace, surrounded by potted plants and flowers. From here, they had a magnificent view of the red-roofed houses of the green and leafy Beya town. The sun was almost fully gone on the horizon, leaving a golden violet hue in the sky as the shadows deepened.

Candles and spotlights twinkled around them. The setting was meant to be romantic. But who was he kidding? All was not well between him and his wife.

This was their third night of eating out here. They'd done it, gone through the motions of eating, barely talking to each other. Oh, they talked. But it was about trivial matters, nothing of true significance.

Neither of them was eating properly. Neither of them was sleeping properly.

As far as he knew, Amara hadn't slept in her bed yet. Every morning for the past three days, he'd found her on the sofa in the living room, tucked into the corner. She seemed to be as miserable as he was.

He took a deep pained breath and closed his eyes as guilt made his chest tight.

Lord knew his intention was not to make her miserable.

Perhaps she was right and he wasn't a good person, wasn't capable of being a good husband if he was making his wife sad three days into their married life.

To everyone else, their life was glorious. Tasteful and graceful photographs from their wedding day had been shared across the official Onyi and Onyia of Beya account announcing their marriage. Fan accounts had sprouted online, and there were now @BeyaSquad and @BeyaStan celebrating and supporting them.

However, Amara had not tweeted since their wedding day when she'd tweeted: *Today is thee day.* But nothing since. She hadn't even retweeted the pictures on the official @TheBeyas account. And she knew about the posts because they had selected the pictures to be shared.

So her lack of social media activities over the past few days told him she was unhappy, as much as her obvious lack of appetite did. They had to talk.

"You haven't said anything about my teaching at Beya High for the week."

He started with the least contentious topic. He'd known she'd come to the school because his bodyguard had seen her on the first day and had told him when the class had ended. He'd expected an argument from her that night. But she'd said nothing. Just sat across him at the table like today, picking at her food.

"Why? So you would say I'm complaining and have another reason to send me home?" She twirled the fork on the plate but didn't pick up anything.

His throat thickened, and he coughed. "That's not true. I'm not looking for reasons to send you home."

"Yeah, right." She didn't look at him and dropped the fork. "Anyway, Lucas told me the school had a teacher shortage, and you were filling in. It's important for the students to get a quality education."

Her acceptance and understanding of his actions floored him, making him feel more guilty. Yes, helping the students was important, and he loved it. But going to the school over the past few days had also been an escape for him.

So he didn't have to face his own inadequacies. That he was failing his wife.

This situation wasn't her fault. She'd been forced to marry him because Zawadi had jilted her. She'd been the wronged party. And expecting her to switch over to him and care about him in only a matter of weeks was unfair to her.

"You speaking your mind is also important," he said, trying to appease her. Hopefully, they could find a middle ground.

"What's the point? You're going to end our marriage in a few weeks' time." She sounded resigned.

He leaned forward, tilting his head so he could see her face properly in the growing shadows. "Amara, don't you see? I don't want to end this marriage. I just want a chance for us to make it work."

"No, I don't see, Zik." She pushed the chair back, making it scrape against the hard floor. "What I see is that you hate me."

"Hate you?" He threw his hands up in the air. "That is farthest thing I feel for you."

"Then how do you explain that for three days, three whole days of living with you, you haven't touched me once. Not once, Zik. What am I? Am I a leper? Unattractive? Not your type? What?"

She finally looked at him, glaring, but the shimmer of tears in her eyes broke his heart.

He took a step towards her, but she shifted away, and he tucked his hands under his armpits to stop from reaching for her again. He couldn't see someone in distress and not seek to comfort them. But she was still withdrawing from him, so physical contact was out of the question. He had to use other methods to soothe her.

Nodding in understanding, he lowered his voice. "You are exactly my type, and I'm very much attracted to you."

Her face puckered, and she gave an unbelieving shake of head. "I'm your type?"

He nodded. "From the tight curls in your hair to the delicate balls of your feet."

She swiped a palm over her natural hair pulled into a bun, a slow smile curling her lips. Perhaps she saw the heated way his gaze followed her movement or the way he tucked in his bottom lip at the corner.

She straightened, seemingly realising the implications. "So why have you done nothing about it?"

He sucked in a deep breath to compose his thoughts.

"Because I'm aware that through the arranged marriage process and Zawadi's abdication, your rights to choose your husband were eroded. You had to marry me, otherwise the public disgrace would have been devastating for you. I understand that. So the last thing I want to do is take away your right to consent to be intimate with me."

"But I married you. Of course I know that sex and intimacy will be part of it." She shifted from one foot to the other, averting her gaze. "Even putting the sex aside. I've been sleeping on that sofa for three nights, and you haven't even tried to carry me to bed once."

He touched his throat, heart racing. Had she been testing him by sleeping on the sofa? He shook his head. She wouldn't stoop so low, would she?

"I wanted to carry you to bed every time I saw you there. But the same issue remains. You don't let me touch you when you're awake. I'm not going to assume consent when you're asleep. That's predatory." He shuddered at the idea of abusing her trust and making a bad situation worse.

"When did I stop you from touching me?" she grumbled, pouting.

"On our wedding night. Right here this evening. You keep jerking back when I reach for you."

She turned away, shaking her head. "A loving husband would carry his wife to bed to make her comfortable. That's not about sex. It's about caring."

He puffed out a breath and nodded. "True. But being a loving husband would imply that we're in a loving relationship. Are we in a loving relationship?"

"I don't know." She walked towards the edge of the terrace.

His heart raced at the possibility in her uncertainty. Could it be that she felt something for him? The reason he'd been so adamant on their wedding night? He didn't want her here purely out of obligations to their parents.

He stood and went to her, swerving to face her. "You don't know? Three days ago, you hated me. Do you feel something different for me now?"

She ignored him for several seconds.

"Amara?" Blood whooshed in his ears.

"Maybe. I don't know." She paced away. "Ever since I saw you teaching in that class, I've had all kinds of confusing feelings. Seeing you teaching kids showed me a side of you I never thought existed, a side that is charitable and serious, that genuinely cares about people. A side that I like."

She liked something about him. A shot of euphoria went through him. He could swear the thumping of his heart would punch a hole through his chest.

"Then I also remember your harsh tone on our wedding night and how you refuse to relent on your ultimatum, which I hate." She walked back towards him. "So yes, I'm confused. I don't know what to do with the contrasting emotions. And by the way, do you want to know why I sleep on the sofa?"

"Why?" he asked tentatively, not wanting anything to dampen the spark of joy within him.

"Because I have panic attacks about having to go home in humiliation at the end of the trial period. I fell asleep in my bed once and woke in cold sweat because I thought I was back in my bedroom at home. The living room is a space where I know you've been in, and it reminds me that I'm in the castle, not at my father's house. So the panic subsides. Also, for some reason, the scent of your blanket relaxes me."

"Thank you so much for telling me."

He took a step towards her, but she raised her hand, stopping him.

"Anyway," she said, tilting her chin up, looking like the haughty princess once more. "Ask for my permission."

"What?" He shook his head, confused about the change in trajectory of the conversation.

"You won't sweep me off my feet or kiss me or make love to me unless I give consent. So ask for the permission to touch me." She sounded snooty and impossible.

His back muscles stiffened, and he had to restrain himself from pulling her across his lap and spanking her ass raw. He was trying so hard to understand her, to adjust to her, but she was constantly thwarting him.

"Are you sure you want to do that?" he asked through a clenched jaw.

"Do what?" She looked at him as if he was being silly.

"Are you sure you want to grant me permission to lay my hands on you?" He left it hanging there so she could read all the implications of his tone.

"You wouldn't dare!" she taunted.

"Wouldn't I?" He raised one brow as he lowered to one knee. "Your Royal Highness, do I have your permission to touch your body?"

She glared at him, not flinching. Oh, she was bold. No doubt.

But he'd waited over ten years for her. Had even given up hope of ever having her like this. Three days ago, it had looked like a lost cause. Like it would never happen. There had been many bonds locking him away from her—his country, parents, brother, and finally, Amara herself. So, he really needed her word. Her consent, and then, every chain, every restraint, would be released from him.

"Permission granted."

Before she'd finished the phrase, he was on his feet and cupping her jaw possessively, not caring that they were on the terrace and would be visible to passing employees. He hesitated only for a moment, savouring the stunned expression on her face.

He teetered on the edge of a cliff. This was it. The moment everything would change, when everything before was shattered and laid to waste. The moment he was free to be himself with her.

He crushed her lips with his, and her moan rumbled through him as he pinned her against the wall. He tilted his head, hardening the kiss, deepening the thrust of his tongue.

Oh, she was his now. No doubt about it. And he was going to relish the claiming.

CHAPTER FOURTEEN

The moment Zik's lips connected with hers, a guttural moan escaped from Amara. Her head spun, her body coming alive like it had never done before. His grip on her chin was firm, yet the cup of his palm on her skin felt gentle. His kiss demanded, and yet, he worshipped her mouth with it.

Everything about this prince, this man, proved contradictory. Since their marriage, he'd elicited conflicting emotions within her. After their argument days ago and he'd ignored her, she'd almost given up about getting physical with him.

Still, it was happening.

She'd never taken Zik seriously. Had never considered him as a lover. He was too unserious, too carefree, too much of a ladies' man. Anyway, she'd had ambitions of being queen, and therefore, her eyes had been on the crown. And the crown had been Zawadi. Until a few months ago.

Then Zik became her husband, and he was going to be her lover. Over the past few days, she'd fantasised about what he would be like as a lover, had yearned to find out why his exes raved about him.

Now, she would find out.

This man who had ignored her for days was kissing her like she belonged to him, his hard, muscled body pressing against her, making her feel his solidity.

She whimpered as the taste of him filled her mouth and his spicy scent permeated her nostrils. Without much thought, her hands rose, curling around his shoulders, clinging onto the taut muscles.

He lit a fire in her veins, heat spreading over her skin. Just from a kiss, and she didn't want it to end.

A groan rumbled through him, vibrating in her chest as his tongue danced with hers. His big hands left her jaw to trail down, until they cupped her bum cheeks, and before she knew it, she'd wrapped her legs around his hips. He didn't break the kiss as he moved, carrying her away from the wall. She clung onto his shoulders, not caring where they were going as long as he never let her go.

She'd always been a good girl. Never had time for bad boys or playboys.

Yet, there was something about the way this sexy, gorgeous playboy prince held her protectively and still caressed her passionately that indicated she would get naughty just for him. Need simmered just beneath the surface, waiting to be set free.

Part of her wanted to confess these feelings to him, to tell him everything. But how could she tell him that she craved him?

He fiddled with a lock, and the door opened. He didn't turn on the light as he carried her farther into the room and then placed her on what felt like a padded table. He stepped away, tugging her bottom lip as he went and leaving her bereft.

Silhouetted by the glow through the glass double doors leading to the terrace, he appeared dark and mysterious, his fiery onyx eyes piercing hers.

"Remember you can always withdraw consent," he said in a growly voice, moving one hand against his wrist as he undid his cufflinks. They tinkled softly as he placed them on a shelf. His eyesight was definitely better than hers, because she still couldn't figure out where they were. Was this his bedroom? Mancave of sorts?

"Why would I?"

Suddenly unsettled, a tremor passed through her, and she felt around, trying to hold onto something solid and met air. She seemed to be on a padded leather stool rather than a chair as she'd first thought.

"Because I'm going to demand everything from you." He rolled up the left sleeve of his white shirt first and did the same for the right arm. Even without the light, the strain of hard pectoral and abdominal muscles against the outfit was visible. "And you may not want to give it to me, babygirl."

It seemed like decades since he'd used the endearment for her. But it had only been days. It suffused her with comforting warmth. Yet, her heartbeat nearly exploded, and the tremors increased. He was talking about sex, right? How demanding could he be? What did he intend for her to do? He wouldn't dare do anything too depraved. They were married.

She swallowed as she tried to work her tongue. "I can handle it."

"Oh, good," he purred and undid the top two buttons of his shirt as he swaggered towards her. "Heaven knows I've wanted you for a long time."

His lips whispered against her earlobe as his hands slid up her bare thighs, pushing her dress up.

His words were like liquid heat between her thighs and made her breathless. "You want me?"

Surely, it was just sex talk, and he was saying it in the heat of the moment. How long could he have wanted her anyway? She'd been betrothed to his brother for over a decade.

"All of you. I've wanted nothing else as much as I want you."

His husky revelation was a shock *and* a shot of arousal, making her core pulse as her nipples hardened. It also gave her a heady boost of power. After she'd spent days agonising over whether he found her attractive or not, now he was confessing to wanting her all along. A part of her wanted to punish him for the misery she'd felt thinking she wasn't good enough for him.

"I can withdraw consent." Her voice wasn't as firm as she'd wanted it to be as his lips brushed her ear and his fingers skimmed her hips.

He leaned back, his teeth flashing white in the dimness, like a shark smelling blood and moving in for the kill. "You can, but you won't. You want me, maybe not as much as I want you, but you do."

He was darn right. She'd waited days for this, for him. She ached for him—her nipples chafed against her bra, and her core throbbed with the rhythm of her heart. Her body tingled, her undies soaked.

So yes, she wanted this infuriatingly sexy man who happened to be her husband of three days. She'd hated him months ago, but now, she desired him. Who knew it was possible?

"You're a jerk, you know." She turned her face away when he tried to kiss her.

"I know, babygirl. You keep reminding me."

His chuckle rumbled against her cheek, making her tremble.

She couldn't suppress the curl of a smile. He was impossible sometimes. But he was also hers, and why should she deny herself what she wanted.

She turned her face in his direction, grabbed his head, and crushed their mouths together. The world spun, and the room tipped and whirled. His tongue invaded her mouth, drawing breath from her, making her melt for him.

She would never classify herself as a noisy lover, but moans were the order of the day with his caresses. His hands worked the dress zipper, and he stepped back, breaking the kiss to her whimper of protest. He tugged the dress high as the thick bulge of his erection pushed against her soaked panties. He groaned, his hips pushing against her.

The sound of his groan was heady even as his finger slid up her thigh and grazed over her crotch, making her skin tingle and whimper.

"Fuck, babygirl. You're wet. For me," he purred, teeth nipping her earlobe.

She flinched at his use of the swear word. It was unexpected, not something she ever expected a well-born prince to say. The filthy word was for commoners.

"Don't use that word. It's dirty," she said even as he caressed her through her undies.

"Oh, didn't you know? I have a very dirty mouth." His tone held humour, and she wasn't sure if he was teasing her or being serious.

"Clean it out … ooohh." She moaned and clutched his body as he continued dragging his finger over her sensitive flesh.

"I bet you won't want my mouth clean when I'm eating your pussy."

As soon as he said the words, the image formed in her mind, and she wanted the reality. Her insides clenched tight, and she tried to pull her legs together.

Zik gripped her thighs, his mouth trailing and nipping the cheek and neck. "Talking about pussy … Spread your thighs, babygirl."

He walked away briefly, leaving her panting and craving more of his touch and kisses. Seconds later, soft glow filled the space from a standing lamp with a cylindrical shade.

The rest of the room came into focus, and her breath hitched. A black piano stood at an angle in the corner, two guitars propped against a wall.

"What is this place?" she couldn't help asking, glancing around.

The rest of the massive space was empty except for the other stool he placed in front of her and lowered his body slowly. He spread his thighs, drawing attention to the bulge in his trousers as he leaned his arms onto his thighs, focusing on her.

"A music room." His gaze dragged over her body like a teasing caress.

"Of course, you used to play." Memories from long ago flashed through her mind. When they'd been younger, teenagers, he and Zediah used to play gigs for them, Zed on the piano and Zik on the guitar. They'd been great. "You still play the guitar?"

"Sometimes. Right now, though, I want to play you." His gaze burned into her, thrilling her. "Show me what's mine, babygirl."

Oh, he was right. He had a dirty mouth. And as much as it appalled her, it thrilled her at the same time, sending heat skittering over her flesh.

The sensible part of her wanted to tell him to piss off. That she wasn't that kind of woman. That she wasn't here for his entertainment.

Yet, something about the rough edge to his voice and the dark possessive way he stared at her stirred a dark ache inside her, evident in the whoosh of blood in her ears, the thundering pulse, the nipples spiking like bullets, and her heavy breasts. Her skin itched to be released from her clothing every time his gaze dragged hungrily over her body. It looked like he wanted to tear her clothes off, and she wondered why he hadn't done it yet.

Just like that, she spread her legs, the hem of her dress riding up, exposing her thighs.

His eyes flared with something fierce. "That's it, babygirl. Pull your panties to the side so I can see your pretty pussy."

Outrage lanced through her, and she clamped her legs shut. "I'm not—"

"You're my wife, and Ikemba wants to eat your pussy. Are you denying me the pleasure of your sweetness, babygirl?"

Ikemba? Why would he say that? Only one person had used that phrase with her. She remembered a night of sensual awakening from so long ago. A blip in her life so she wasn't going there.

Still, her entire body flashed hot, and her core clenched tight. Moreover, this was Zik, and he was her husband. It didn't matter if this was his thing. She wanted his mouth on her like he'd promised.

Slowly, she spread her leg, anchoring her feet on the stand so they didn't dangle, and tugged the seam of her undies aside. She wished she'd worn a sexy thong like on their wedding night instead of these lace French knickers.

It didn't seem to matter, though, because his gaze ate her up, and he shifted his stool closer.

"So fucking perfect." He reached up and cupped her face, kissing her deeply. Then he was on his knees, between her thighs, removing her shoes before lifting her legs over his shoulders. "Relax against the piano, babygirl. We're about to make music."

His breath whispered on her thigh, teasing her bare folds, sending tremors through her. His mouth grazed her, the sensation knocking her back against the piano keys, and she cried out along with the musical note. He tongued her opening, pushing deep. Then he traced the tip up, parting her soft folds and pressing over her clit.

He growled, harmonising with her moans and the depressed piano. His mouth covered her core, his tongue swirling over her clit.

Gasping, she got lost in sensation, threw her head back, closed her eyes. Her hands flew behind her, palms flat on the piano keys, making sweet music just like he did with her body.

Zik continued tonguing her folds, tasting her, awakening every nerve ending. He groaned and pushed fingers into her, working her body to a frenzy.

Moans tumbled out of her, toes curling into his back, her body writhing as a powerful orgasm ripped through her.

She was half-aware of moving as Zik lifted her against the wall. He eased the head of his erection against her opening, teasing her and rubbing it up and down. She leaked sticky wetness all over his length until it dripped along the thick, veined shaft as he slowly stroked himself and then the solid erection slammed into her.

"Oooohhhh," she cried out, arching off the wall.

He swallowed it with a kiss, making her taste herself, a forbidden naughty experience.

"Fuck, babygirl. You make me so hard." The husky tone of his voice indicated he walked on a razor's edge. His palm cupped her cheek gently, and when his gaze met her, he rocked her world with the soft and tender expression. "Being with you, touching you, tasting you, being inside you, all of it is perfection."

He kissed her again, so intensely she felt it in her toes. He started stroking in and out of her, a palm squeezing her breast, the other gripping her hip. He was thick, making her feel full and amazing. He'd just given her an intense orgasm, but her body caught fire again, arousal rising. This gorgeous man drove her insane.

"I want you to come with me. Can you do that for me, babygirl? Touch yourself." He sucked the flesh on her neck.

On any other day, she might have refused. But with the incredible way he made her feel, lowering her hand between their bodies and rubbing her clit seemed the most natural thing at the moment.

"That's it." He pumped into her deeper, faster.

Perhaps it was a combination of everything, the sound of his groans, the feel of his shaft inside her, his taste in her mouth. Soon, the fever was chasing over her skin and exploding in her core. He kissed her hard, his thickness pulsing inside her as he came.

Panting, they clung to each other, and he placed soft kisses all over her sweaty face before pulling back and gazing into her eyes.

"You're mine now, babygirl."

His deep, warm voice enveloped her like a blanket, making her feel protected and needed.

For some reason, his claim made her happy, and she smiled. "And you're mine, too, Ikemba."

They both froze. She hadn't meant to say the endearment, but it seemed suitable for their dynamic and what they'd just shared.

His gaze became heated and possessive as a slow grin spread on his face while he brushed damp hair away from her temple. "I'm yours, and Ikemba is going to enjoy taking care of his babygirl. Now, hold on tight, let me take you somewhere more comfortable."

Glad she didn't have to use her weak legs, she clung on, her face tucked into his neck as he straightened his clothes and hers before existing the music room.

For the first time since she'd agreed to marry Zik, she felt positive about her decision. Perhaps she'd married the correct brother.

CHAPTER FIFTEEN

"Before you go, just a reminder that your Business Studies teacher will be back next week," Zik announced, and the class of masked Year 12 students at Beya High School cheered and drummed on their desks. He raised his hand, and they quietened. "But that also means I won't be here."

Murmurs followed a brief silence before someone said, "Why don't you stay and become our teacher?"

Zik laughed along with some of the students. He sat on the edge of the table, facing the class. He'd thoroughly enjoyed the five days he'd spent educating the Years 11 and 12 students in preparation for their Secondary School Certificate Examinations.

Usually, once every year, he taught at his Youth Leadership Program where some of the best students in the country and beyond attended a weeklong seminar hosted at Beya High. He invited some of the top African experts in different fields to participate and lecture. So he was used to teaching.

However, when he'd spoken to Principal Bene earlier in the week and she'd indicated the school was short-staffed, he had volunteered to cover since he didn't have any official engagements for the period.

While he'd worked to ensure that laptops were delivered to every secondary school and university student in Bagumi during the pandemic, not all of them had access to stable internet connectivity. So remote learning and home schooling wasn't available to every child.

"Because he is the crown prince," another student chimed in. "And will be the king of Bagumi one day."

"That's not finalised yet," Zik said, pressing a hand to his stomach as the dismay he'd felt returned to burn a hole in his insides. "I'm only the interim crown prince. The king and the parliament will decide who becomes the future king."

"But Prince Zawadi abdicated. Who else could it be?" another student commented.

A smile curled Zik's mouth. These young people were good for his ego. "I have three other brothers, you know?"

Just then, his bodyguard stepped away from the door and approached. He leaned over and whispered. "The Onyia is here."

Zik straightened, a thrill shooting through him at the prospect of seeing his wife. After the first time she'd visited the school unannounced but had left without speaking to him, he told the bodyguard to inform him ASAP if she showed up again at the premises.

"Excuse me a moment," he said to the class and strutted to the door, unable to contain his excitement. He hadn't planned on seeing his wife until later this evening.

Sure enough, Amara sashayed along the veranda in his direction, trailed by another royal bodyguard. She wore a short-sleeved abstract orange and navy geometric print maxi dress, her feet in multi-coloured suede slingbacks matching her dress. Even when she was being casual, she still looked like a catwalk model princess. Her eyes sparkled, her smile beautiful to beckon.

Adrenaline rushed through him, and his pulse accelerated. He hurried towards her.

"Onyi." Her bodyguard bowed deep.

Zik acknowledged him with a nod, but his gaze didn't leave Amara's face as he stepped into her space, cupped her cheek, and pressed his lips to the corner of hers briefly after pushing down her face mask. "This is a pleasant surprise, babygirl."

The sound of giggling and murmuring made him realise the teenagers were watching through the open windows.

"I thought we could have a picnic for lunch," Amara said, lowering her gaze in a shy smile.

He loved her smile. Loved knowing he contributed to its existence, considering how their married life had started out and the tumultuous emotional rollercoaster of the past week.

They said, 'a week is a long time in politics.' But it also seemed a long time in marriage, too.

First had been the high of the wedding ceremony followed by the heated argument in the car on the way back from the airport. Next had been three days of depression until they'd had the revealing conversations which led to a night of making love. And the tide turned.

That had been two days ago, and they'd had bliss since. Yes, he'd had to attend Beya High yesterday and today to complete the work he'd volunteered to do. However, he'd been looking forward to their nights together. They seemed bent on making up for the lost time.

This woman who'd hated him only days ago was now planning picnics with him like they were a normal couple in love. He'd almost given up hope this would happen and knew this didn't mean that everything had been resolved between them—his ascension to the throne or lack thereof a major part of it.

Still, he would accept the little blessings because they seemed far between these days.

"Thank you." He grinned, palms cupping her shoulders. "Since you're here, let me introduce you to the class, otherwise they won't quieten down."

She laughed, lifting the face covering which matched her dress over her mouth and nose. "Okay."

"Oh, you might have to keep the mask off for the speech-to-text application. Unfortunately, it doesn't work very well with the face coverings unless you're wearing a mic. There are two hard-of-hearing students."

"It's not a problem. I can sign."

"You can?" He blinked in disbelief.

"Yes. My cousin is deaf so we had to learn to communicate with him."

How did he not know that about her? So much he didn't know; so much he yearned to find out about her.

He took her hand and returned to the class. The students who'd been standing by the windows hustled back to the seats.

"Settle down, please," he said as they stood in front of the class.

Amara tried to tug her hand free. But he held on, meeting her confused gaze with a smile.

He understood her confusion. Bagumian royal protocols, which she'd been tutored in, forbade public displays like handholding and kissing. He supposed she'd never held hands with Zawadi when they'd been engaged. At least, Zik had never seen any physical contact between them.

His chest tightened, and he forced his mind away from thinking about whatever they'd done in private. He'd promised to leave the past in the past. But sometimes... He shook his head.

"I'd like to present my wife, Princess Amara, the Onyia of Beya," he said to the quiet, standing class and released his wife's hand so she could sign.

"Good afternoon, Onyia," the students chorused.

"Good afternoon, students," Amara replied, moving her hands and fingers as she spoke. "It's wonderful meeting you. I hope my husband is a good teacher to you."

"Of course I am," Zik replied, with a huge grin. His wife had depths he hadn't realised—the humour, the sign language, her innate albeit innocent sexiness.

"He is, Your Highness. We want him to come back next week. Maybe he could become our teacher full-time."

"No," another student said. "He should become the king so he will make sure there are quality teachers for all the students in Bagumi."

"Wow. I definitely support the Onyi to become the future king." Amara glanced at Zik before turning back to the students.

A girl sitting in front raised her hand.

"What's your name?" Amara asked.

"My name is Dimi," the girl replied.

"Lovely name, Dimi. Do you have a question?"

"Yes. I would like to know why there isn't a crown princess."

"Duh, because women don't inherit the throne," a boy responded.

"Why not?" the same girl retorted. "Women are great leaders."

"That's very true," Amara said before Zik could respond. "In ancient Bagumi law, women were allowed to succeed the throne and rule as queens. As you may have already studied in history, Bagumi had women queens, and Queen Obiong is a famous warrior queen who defeated her rivals to claim the throne in the 1500s. In those days, siblings could challenge each other for the throne. However, much later, the law was changed banning the siblings challenge and introducing first male succession. The princesses were expected to marry and focus on their family lives rather than ruling the kingdom."

As he watched Amara interact with the students, Zik's heart filled with joy. Although he had doubts about whether she would stay with him long-term, he delighted in seeing this friendly, personable side to her. Not just the online persona of abrasive internet warrior. Maybe they could find a middle ground beyond sex. Although the sex was awesome. Damn, his heart rate accelerated thinking about it.

The bell sounded, interrupting his heated musings, and ending the class conversations.

He straightened. "Thank you for being great students and keep up the good work."

"Thank you, sir," the class chorused.

"Class dismissed."

The place erupted in activity as the students packed up and left.

When the room was empty except for him and Amara and the bodyguards outside, he leaned against the desk and tugged her between his legs. He couldn't resist touching her. It had been too many hours without her today.

She yelped in surprise and averted her face when he removed her mask and tried to kiss her. "Zik, this is inappropriate."

"Inappropriate? How? I'm trying to kiss my wife in an empty classroom." He grinned, imagining all the other things he could do to her in this space.

"The royal handbook on protocols and etiquette explicitly forbids any kind of physical contact in public places. It breaches the decency laws. You've already kissed me outside and held my hand in front of the class. Let's not make it worse."

Damn. She was quoting the royal handbook now? He tilted his head. "Does it bother you when I touch you in public?"

"No, it doesn't, but I worry about what people will think. You are the Crown Prince. People have certain expectations of you." She looked serious, and some of the old Amara returned. The proper princess.

"You know, if I had the option of giving up touching you or giving up the crown prince position, I'd give up the crown."

"You can't be serious." Her eyes bulged.

He accepted that this could be uncomfortable for her. She wasn't used to PDAs. So he didn't drag it out. "I am. But I'll stop touching you in public since it makes you uncomfortable. Where is the picnic? I'm starving."

"Lucas has it all set up. Follow me." Amara walked towards the door, but her brows furrowed.

Zik didn't like it, and he halted. "Why are you frowning?"

She glanced at him and averted her gaze.

"Tell me." He tickled her waist. "Or I'm going to kiss you thoroughly right here."

She giggled, trying to get out of reach. "Okay. Okay ... I was just wondering why the idea of you not touching me in public made me sad. Then I realised your touches show that you need me."

She didn't know the half of it. He needed her like he'd never needed anything else. The notion of this thing between them coming to an end one day scared him more than he was willing to admit.

"I do. I need you." Touching her was like a salve to the wound which had festered for years when she'd been betrothed to his brother.

She stepped close, looked him deep in the eyes, and cupped his hairy chin. His heart somersaulted.

"It feels great to be needed," she said in a low voice, her breath feathering his lips. "I don't want to lose that. But I also don't want us to get into trouble. So let's minimise the public display, especially when we return to Darusa in a few days."

"Okay. For you and only for you, I will." He lifted her hand and kissed her knuckles.

"Oh, you're impossible." She giggled, sashaying out of the class. "Come on. Let's go and eat."

The sway of her hips had him hardening on the spot. "I'm definitely hungry."

"No. It's not that kind of food," she replied without looking back.

He chuckled, and hope sparked within him. His wife was beginning to understand him.

CHAPTER SIXTEEN

October 2020, Bagumi

Amara sat on the sofa in the Safari Room, sitting upright, hands clasped on her lap, legs crossed and tucked to the side in the correct posture for a royal princess.

She and Zik had arrived in Darusa two weeks ago. So much had happened. And for a new wife, the changes to her life would seem like a baptism of fire. There'd been news conferences, a dinner in their honour, and other social engagements designed for Zik to show off his new bride.

She'd expected a lot of it, considering she'd been preparing to marry Zawadi for a decade.

However, what she hadn't expected was the way Zik made her feel. Yes, the sex was out of this world and explosive. But it was the moments in between—the soft expressions when he looked at her, the gentle caresses when he touched her, and the way he reassured her when she was uncertain—those moments caught her off-guard.

Seemingly, all it had needed was for her to give permission and the big, athletic, former party boy became tender and loving. He didn't miss the opportunity to touch her even in fleeting moments—a feathery caress or a firm hold keeping her grounded.

All their online banter before they'd gotten married, the annoyance she'd felt each time she'd seen a photo of him with another woman, began to make sense.

Zawadi had barely paid her any attention. He'd never responded to any of her online posts—he didn't have a personal account and their offline contact had been minimal to once a week max.

However, Zik had often responded to her online. Even when it had been snarky she'd craved the interaction. Sometimes she even went looking for trouble by tweeting something directly related to him.

Perhaps subconsciously, then, she'd wanted Zik's attention to herself. Because he gave himself readily. No reservations. In a weird way, he'd been there for her online, supporting her, rebuking her, teasing her.

Now, this proved a problem. How could she believe that a man who'd spent years swinging from one woman to another would settle with her? Would he get bored with her one day like he did with others?

Her husband was highly sexed. No doubt about it. And he seemed to have sparked the sex craze within her, too.

She yearned for him, looked forward to any opportunity to be with him.

A recent example of their erotic escapades flashed in her mind from the night of the family dinner.

***

Zik had explained that although Amara knew most of them, tradition dictated she be formally introduced to everyone. That evening they left their apartment in DP hand-in-hand. They could maintain physical contact until they reached the venue.

When she spotted the uniformed guards outside the family banquet hall, she halted, making Zik stop too.

"You, okay?" He tilted his head to study her face, looking dapper in his tuxedo suit.

Warmth bloomed in her chest as butterflies fluttered in her belly. "I just wanted to let you know in case I forget later. You take my breath away."

His lips curled into the most gorgeous smile as his dark eyes glimmered with heat. "Thank you, babygirl. And in case I don't tell you later, you are the belle of the ball."

He leaned down and kissed the corner of her lips, like he did sometimes, making her skin tingle. Even better, the butterfly caress didn't smudge her lipstick.

She wore a white ruffle-neck long-sleeved blouse tucked into a black-and-white-patterned, maxi, ball skirt trailing over her black diamante stilettos, her hair coiffed into a fashionable up-do by the stylist.

"Thank you." She beamed up at him. "Just remember to rescue me before midnight."

"Your prince is always prepared to rescue you." He winked and straightened. "You ready?"

She swallowed, clasping her hands in front of her. "Yes."

They stepped to the double doors and stopped outside. Zik nodded at the head of palace operations, a middle-aged man named Hammed, who stepped inside and announced them.

"Presenting The Onyi and Onyia of Beya, His Royal Highness, Interim Crown Prince Azikiwe dan Ibrahim Saene and Her Royal Highness, Princess Amara Azikiwe Saene."

They entered the glittering hall where his siblings waited in a receiving line of couples. The men were in tuxedos or suited in black ties while the women wore formal outfits in the black and white theme.

At the head of the column were Zawadi and Danai.

Zik glanced at her. She smiled, hoping to reassure him. For the first time since his oldest brother jilted her, Amara didn't hold any resentment towards the man. In fact, she hadn't thought much about her ex after the night she made love with Zik in the castle music room.

"Amara, I'd like to present my first brother, Zawadi, and his partner, Danai," Zik said and stepped towards the couple.

"Congratulations to both of you," Zawadi and Danai said, almost together, their expressions guarded.

"Thank you for joining us tonight," Amara replied sincerely, although she remained grateful about the rule banning physical contact. It meant they couldn't shake hands or embrace the others.

"Thank you for gifting Zik to me," she said to Danai while Zawadi chatted with Zik.

"What do you mean?" the woman asked, her posture stiff.

"If you weren't with Zawadi, I wouldn't have Zik. He is the best."

She said it so Danai would know she was over Zawadi. But it was true, too.

Zik was fun and attentive in a way Zawadi had never been. They communicated, often, via any means—social media, in person, phone messages. It was amazing to see how different the brothers were.

Amara reached out and instinctively, Zik found her hand and held it, although he wasn't looking directly at her. She wasn't supposed to touch him, but she wanted to reassure him and herself with the contact. This showed how in tune they were with each other, seeking each other out without too much thought. And secure in knowing the other person would be there.

As they moved down the line, none of the other couples were holding hands. Amara loosened her grip, and Zik released her.

Next were the latest Saene couple, Kalahari and Edina. Kalahari reminded her of Zareb in personality, and Edina seemed lovely.

At dinner, she was seated between Isha and Riona on the wives and female siblings round table with white blossoms in a narrow glass centrepiece and a dangling chandelier above them. Zik sat with the male spouses and princes on a different table with similar decorations. They were served a five-course meal with champagne.

Afterwards, the siblings and spouses gathered in one of the reception rooms to chat. Midway through the evening, she received a text message from Zik.

A chọrọ m gị. Meet me in the winter garden.

That could only mean one thing. Her core clenched. She needed him, too, sitting here wondering when they would get some privacy. But she hadn't expected his message tonight. Although he liked sending her naughty notes in Igbo language. Her cheeks heated as she sent a reply.

We can't leave. These are our guests.

They'll hardly notice we're gone for 30 mins. Make an excuse to use the ladies and go. I'll meet you there in five.

Pulse skyrocketing, she glanced in Zik's direction, but he didn't look at her. He seemed immersed in what Zain was saying to him.

"Excuse me a moment," she said to Isha who nodded. She left the reception room and headed into the well-lit corridors past stationary guards and then through a side door into the darkness of the gardens.

She knew this palace very well, having spent a lot of time here as a child, running around, playing hide and seek.

This gave her an idea when she unlocked the doors and stepped into the cold conservatory housing the temperate climate plants. She ignored the table and chairs and went to the trellis with hanging ivy which obscured the view from the door.

A minute or so later, the door squeaked, and footsteps announced an arrival.

"Babygirl, are you hiding?"

His voice was molten chocolate, and her heart rate spiked.

"I am. Find me, and you can claim me," she teased, looking forward to an adult hide and seek.

"Oh, it's a treasure hunt. I'm game. I look forward to claiming the prize." He sounded amused.

"You're going to have to catch me first." She placed her hand on her chest, trying to calm her racing pulse as she listened for his footsteps and shuffled along the rows.

"You know when I find you, I'm going to bend you over the garden table and fuck you." He sounded close.

"Promises, promises," she said in a breathless voice she didn't recognise. When did she become this brazen about her sex life?

She shuffled backwards, ran into a solid wall, and swivelled.

Zik stood there, all six foot and change of him, looking impeccable in the black tailored tuxedo, crisp white shirt, and bow tie. He stood so close, his spicy cologne scenting the air. In the dim light, his broad shoulders rolled beneath the suit jacket.

Lord, she could lick him right now, eat him all up.

Get a grip, woman.

Zik took a deep breath, his chest expanding. His glittering eyes trailed down the length of her body. "Gotcha!"

"You got me. What are you going to do with me?" Her skin tingled, and anticipation gathered into a ball in her stomach, ready to explode.

Zik was like a drug in her vein, a powerful drug she couldn't seem to resist. Did he feel the same about her? Or was she just a passing fancy?

He cocked his head as if studying her face. Then he straightened and watched her silently. Seconds later, she realised their breathing was in sync. He did that sometimes when he noticed she was anxious.

He was so good at reading her body language and responding accordingly even when she was being non-verbal. Another amazing aspect of their relationship.

"We don't have to make love. Being with you here is as rewarding," he said in a soothing voice.

She swivelled and headed towards the table, her core pulsing between her legs. "I love the sentiments, Ikemba. But I want what you promised."

His fingers brushed her cheek, and his hand threaded the hair on her nape. His touch sparked a wildfire inside her, the anticipation exploding to send fireworks that ignited every nerve ending in her body. He exhaled heavily, a low growl she'd heard several times.

This feeling he evoked had to be dangerous because, look at them: they were about to desecrate one of Queen Zulekha's favourite places. She would have a fit if she found out what they were about to do.

And this was the new Amara, revelling in the wildness Zik unleashed in her.

"Omalicha, do I have permission to fuck you?" His breath whispered against her nape.

The endearment caught her off-guard, even as the obscenity rankled. This was the dichotomy of emotions she battled with daily where he was concerned. She should be pissed off with him.

Yet, a warm shiver travelled down her spine, pooling between her thighs. He was charming and sexy, to her annoyance. Not to mention the moments when he was tender and considerate. Now, she struggled to find reasons to refuse him anything even when he was being crude.

She was supposed to be the sensible one, the opposite of Zik's impulsiveness. Yet, as she opened her mouth, only one reply escaped her parched throat. "Yes."

His thumb brushed against her cheek. Then, he was tilting her face and claiming her mouth with a groan. His other fingers fiddled with the front buttons of her blouse, seeming as impatient as her for the skin-to-skin contact.

She gasped as he squeezed her exposed breast, his mouth demanding and setting her ablaze. She shuffled back, rolling her bum against his groin.

He released her mouth with a groan. "I can't keep my hands off you."

"I don't want you to stop touching me." He was hers and she was his, right here, right now. These moments with him chased away her fears about their future. The lust between them was a massive electrical storm, crackling and popping.

He turned her to face the table, and she reached out, gripping the edge. Then his hands were tugging up her skirt and shoving her undies aside.

She shivered as pressure built between her legs while his fingers teased and caressed, driving sane thoughts from her mind. She chased the orgasm throbbing through her until it exploded into a crescendo, making her dizzy.

His rock-hard erection then pressed against her, poised at her entrance, letting her get used to his presence. But she didn't want to wait, and she slammed backwards as he gripped her hips, holding her still.

"So impatient, babygirl." He leaned over her, chuckling and pressing kisses to her earlobe and nape.

Then he thrust hard, his thickness stretching her like it always did. Her body rocked forward and back, the rhythm swaying the table on the spot.

She bit her bottom lip, holding back her cries of pleasure when he reached down and stroked her clit.

He paused, letting her catch her breath before driving into her with force, shoving her flat on the table as her orgasm happened in a flash of freak storm, bursting through her and weakening her legs.

He caught her, his arm around her waist, keeping her upright as he continued thrusting until he came inside her, his body covering hers, his lips on her neck.

Spent, she floated on a weightless cloud of euphoria.

How could something so right be classified as wrong?

***

"Mrs Zik, the queens are here."

Lucas's words woke her from her daydream.

Amara jerked upright, straightening just as Zawadi's mother and Zik's mother entered the reception room.

"Your Graces." She curtsied deep, glad to hide her face and recover from the embarrassment of nearly being caught playing back the lovemaking session she'd had with Zik in the first queen's winter garden.

How did Zik get so deep in her head to even take over her waking hours? Next, it would be her heart. Could she trust him, considering his past?

"Rise, Amara," Zawadi's mother said in a stiff voice.

Amara wondered if she knew what they'd done. She suppressed a groan, hoping not. The garden had been enclosed and dark. They'd kept the noise to a minimum, and she had used the ladies to tidy up afterwards so that she didn't look different when she re-joined the party. Zik had been in the lounge when she'd returned, so hopefully, no one had noticed their absence.

Still...

"How are you?" Zik's mother asked, examining her with a smile as she sat on the settee next to Amara. Always attentive and compassionate, the woman was the most loving mother-in-law Amara could wish for and such a huge contrast to the stern first consort. Another reason she celebrated her marriage to Zik instead of Zawadi.

"I am well, thank you." She resettled on the spot she'd chosen previously.

Another woman came in behind the queens. She was older, probably in her forties or fifties, in a hijab and face covering.

"This is Salima. She will be taking over as your assistant," Queen Zulekha announced as she settled onto another sofa.

Amara frowned. "Thank you, Your Grace. It's kind of you to assign someone to me. But I was hoping to recruit my staff and interview them myself before the appointment. In the meantime, I have Lucas."

"That may be so. But Lucas is male, and it is inappropriate for you to spend so much time with him. You're a married woman. The wife to the interim crown prince. You have to live to standards above all the other wives."

Hang on a minute. Did she just imply that Amara would have an affair with Lucas?

She opened her mouth, then clamped it shut when Queen Sapphire nudged her with an elbow. During their first week at Darusa Palace, Queen Sapphire had warned her to not ruffle any feathers because Zik was on trial as crown prince. Therefore, anything Amara did or said would reflect on him.

Queen Zulekha stared at her as if daring her to complain.

Sure, she would have like to recruit her assistant. But it wasn't a deal breaker. So, she composed herself and smiled at the new assistant. "It's nice to meet you, Salima."

"Thank you, Your Highness. I look forward to working with you," the woman replied, still standing.

"Same here. Please take a seat."

Salima sat on an armchair farther out.

"This brings me to the other item to discuss," Queen Zulekha said. "You were informed to close your personal social media pages. But it was brought to my attention that you still have them running. Why?"

Amara stiffened. This was a huge bone of contention. "I discussed the matter with my husband, and we agreed to keep our personal profiles along with the official Onyi and Onyia of Beya accounts."

"That's inappropriate. You were allowed some grace period which is over now. Hand over the details to Salima, and she will work on getting them deactivated immediately."

Amara's spine stiffened. That was not happening. She'd fought hard to build those social media pages until she had millions of followers. The accounts were her voice online. She used it to advocate for women's rights issues and anything else that caught her attention. Like the current situation in Nigeria and the ongoing ENDSARS protests against police brutality.

"Your Grace, that's going to be impossible. As you are aware there are protests going on in Nigeria? Young people have been harassed by the police for a long time. I'm using those pages to highlight the issues and boost the voices of the protesters. I have millions of followers who share my posts. The world needs to know what's going on. You can't close them down. It's too important."

"You are married to a Bagumian prince. You should focus your energy on local matters." The woman sounded impatient. "If you need to issue formal statements about the problems in Nigeria, the palace communications team will draft them for you."

More like issuing thoroughly sanitised statements which will have none of Amara's heart or soul. Suppressing her frustration, she tried to hold back the growl bubbling.

"Get those accounts closed by the end of the week. That's my final word on the matter." Queen Zulekha got up and left the room.

"Salima, please leave us," Queen Sapphire said.

"Your Grace. Your Highness." Salima bowed and left the room, shutting the door.

When it was just the two of them, Amara turned to Zik's mother, unable to keep silent any longer. "Mum, surely, you can see my point. Nigeria is in my DNA, and this issue matters to me. I can't ignore it."

"I know. But we must tread carefully and play smart. I know a thing or two about protests and disrupting the status quo. I protested South Africa's Apartheid regime and against the murder of Thomas Sankara of Burkina Faso."

"Wow. Really?" Amara's mouth dropped open.

"Sure. I know you young ones like to think that you invented protests, especially considering what's going on in the world this year. But we did it, long before social media existed. We were revolutionaries and wanted to change the world. But I believe the most significant way to change to world is through my children. I raised them to be critical thinkers, to analyse situations and question everything. To make up their own minds. Of course, it means that sometimes, they get into trouble, especially in a conservative country like Bagumi. But if they never push the boundaries, things will never change."

Amara puffed out a breath of relief. The woman echoed her thoughts. Zik's mother had a quiet intelligence which could easily be mistaken for compliance and docility. Amara was beginning to learn the queen was fierce and the meekness deceptive.

"That is so true, Mum. But what should I do about the social media accounts? I really can't close them down."

"Well, it seems to me that if your million social media followers were to find out about the threat of closure to your accounts, they would protest on your behalf, and the powers that be will have no option but to leave your accounts alone. Freedom of speech is a Bagumian right, and you are not exempt." Queen Sapphire patted her hand and stood, smiling. "You didn't hear that from me. Give my love to Azikiwe. And thank you for putting the bounce back in his step."

She winked and sashayed out of the room, leaving Amara in a daze of wonder.

Zik's mother was badass. But what did she mean by putting the bounce back in Zik's step?

CHAPTER SEVENTEEN

"This is unfair." Amara paced their living room floor. "How can they ban peaceful protests? People should have the right to agitate."

Zik sat on the sofa watching her. It was late in the evening, and he'd had a long day already—back-to-back meetings discussing the pandemic, the future of Bagumi, and the recent protests.

But his wife's agitation kept him fully present. He didn't like seeing her upset. "I think they want to stop it from escalating."

Protests had erupted in Bagumi following the ones in Nigeria. The Nigerian community in Bagumi had been picketing the Nigerian Consulate in Darusa, calling for the Nigerian government to take action against the police force members abusing their powers.

However, certain people in Bagumi had used the opportunity to raise xenophobic sentiments. They claimed that Nigerians were invading their country, taking their jobs, dazzling their women. Some Nigerian business had even been attacked.

Now, parliament wanted to ban all the protests.

"If they want to stop it from escalating, they should focus their efforts on finding the people attacking Nigerian-owned businesses in Bagumi." She threw her hands up in the air. "Isn't it bad enough that Queen Zulekha wants to close my social media accounts so I can't advocate for the protesters in Nigeria? Now, this. If I didn't know this family well, I'd think they hated Nigerians."

Zik's chest squeezed tight. Amara wasn't wrong. There seemed to be a sudden hatred for all things Nigeria rearing its ugly head amongst certain circles. But he knew why. It was because of him. Because some people didn't want him to become the future king.

"By the way, your mother is fierce. Now I understand where Isha got hers. But I swear Zawadi's mother hates me. The woman has been so cold since I arrived. I don't even understand it. She was the one who wanted me to marry into this family. And it wasn't my fault that Zawadi fell in love with someone else. Yet, it feels like she is penalising me for it. That's just so unfair. I mean, how am I supposed to become the future queen if I can't even express my opinions? Is that the kind of wife you want?"

"Of course not." He sighed as guilt ramped up through him. He had to come clean. "Babygirl, please sit. There's something I need to tell you."

Frowning, she walked over and settled on the sofa beside him. "What is it?"

He pushed off the sofa, needing to keep some distance so he could think. Otherwise, he would grab her and make love to her. But it wouldn't solve the problem. She needed to know the truth about his position.

They'd come a long way and had become attuned to each other's needs. But he also realised this could be a deal-breaker.

"I know why there seems to be a sudden hatred for all things Nigerian in Bagumi," he said, running a hand over his head. He hated that he brought this stress onto her. "It's because of me. Because you're married to me, and you're Nigerian."

"You? How?"

"The marriage contract between our families states that the Onoh princess would marry the Saene Crown Prince. However, when Zawadi..." he paused to pick the right words because he didn't want to say jilted you. "When Zawadi abdicated, the crown prince position should have automatically come to me. As you're aware, I'm only the Interim Crown Prince."

"Yes, and that's because Kalahari is contending for the throne."

"That is not entirely correct. Before Kalahari got onto the scene, I was already informed that I was unsuitable to be the future king. Demonising Nigerians is a political ploy to make sure I don't become the future king because I'm married to one."

"Pardon? Why not? You were next in line and the king's son."

Zik inhaled hard. "Yes, I am. But Queen Zulekha said I was unsuitable because of my sex life. She actually called me the 'whore of Bagumi' right in from of Danai, Zawadi, and my parents."

Amara gasped.

"She did what? Is that woman deranged? How could she?" Her fury was visible as she got of the sofa, paced a few steps, then turned to him. "I'm so sorry she said that to you. She had no right."

He was so shocked, he had to do a double-take. "Did you hear what I said? She called me a whore, which is the exact opinion you had about me before we got married, right?"

She averted her gaze, looking shamefaced. "Yes, I did. I'm not proud of it. I judged you based on superficial things. Come to think of it, a lot of it was based on comparisons to Zawadi. She liked to remind me of how Zawadi was pious, which you weren't. He was disciplined and responsible and consistent, and you weren't those things according to her."

Zik flinched. Did she still have feelings for Zawadi? It hadn't seemed that way when they'd all met up for the dinner party a few days ago. In fact, that evening, while they'd walked down the introducing line and paused to chat with Danai and his brother, Amara had extended her hand towards him, and he'd grabbed it and squeezed. Perhaps she'd been seeking comfort, but he'd also been reassured in that contact.

"But none of that matters because you don't have to be like Zawadi. Piety doesn't make for a great king, necessarily. We all know your father wasn't pious. Kalahari is the evidence. And yes, you're spontaneous and fun, which is anathema to

Zawadi. But I love that about you. You're also responsible, compassionate, protective. You care deeply about people in a way I've never seen Zawadi do so. Zawadi cared because it was his duty to care. You do it because you love to do it. All those things make you a great candidate for the crown."

He glanced around the place, because there had to be someone else here she was referring to. But alas, there were only two of them.

"Are you talking about me? Because I swear you are describing someone else."

She stepped up to him and swatted his chest. "Of course I'm talking about you. And that's the other thing. You feel unworthy of the crown. I can see it in your demeanour. This is something I would never have seen if I hadn't married you. I always saw you as cocky, but beneath all that swagger, you're quite a sensitive soul."

"Damn, the secret is out," he joked, trying to cover the scary truth.

She saw through him and it scared him that she could unravel him in only a matter of weeks. He had nowhere to run, nowhere to hide, excerpt in her arms. He leaned down to kiss her as a distraction.

She pulled away, smiling as if she could see his ploy. "No sexing until we talk through this."

He sighed knowing there would be no reprieve for him. "Yes, Your Highness."

She cocked her hip and eyebrow, and he chuckled, settling back on the sofa.

"I'm serious." She sat down beside him again. "Why do you feel unworthy of the throne?"

He shrugged. "I don't know. I've spent my whole life knowing Zawadi was going to be king. I never wanted it. Then when the position could become mine, my stepmother rejected the idea, and my father didn't seem enthusiastic about it. A part of me feels that maybe they're right. Maybe I'm not suitable. So perhaps it should pass to Zediah or Kalahari or whoever wants it."

Shaking her head, she took his right hand, cupping it between her dainty ones. "Ikemba, gee m ntị, listen to me. This is the exact reason you should be king. The crown should not be for those hungry for power, which was Kalahari's motivation, or for those doing it out of duty, which is Zawadi's motivation. It should be for those with the heart of a king, which is you. Your father is a good king for his time. But the future is ours, and we want a different kind of leadership. We want leaders who understand the future and are ready to adapt. Not those who will tie us to the past. You are that person. That leader."

Blown away by Amara's words, Zik reverted to a bad habit, dismissing it with a joke because she couldn't really be telling him the truth. She couldn't really be saying he was good enough to be king.

"Sounds like you should be the monarch instead," he teased.

"Maybe when you become king and die, then I can become the monarch," she retorted, swatting him hard several times.

"Hey, you're already thinking about killing me off." He laughed, reaching for her.

"Yes, because you're impossible. I'm trying to be serious, and you keep joking." She shifted away and crossed her arms over her chest, sulking.

"Okay. I'll behave." He slipped off the sofa to his knees in front of her, clasping her thighs. "Omalicha, ngwa ndo. Biko."

She loved it when he spoke Igbo to her. As expected, her frown thawed, and a reluctant smile brightened her face.

He tugged her arm and pressed a kiss to her knuckles. "You know I don't like seeing you upset."

"Then stop upsetting me." She pouted, adorably. "I'm trying to tell you something important. You might not believe in yourself. But I believe in you."

He clutched her palm to his chest so she could feel the steady beat of his heart. "So you think I will make a good king."

"Not just a good one. A great king. An awesome one."

"Even though people see me as promiscuous and unserious."

"That's because it's all you've allowed people to see of you. They don't see the hard work you put in within the communities. They don't see you volunteering to teach in a high school during your honeymoon. They don't see you making sacrifices so others will shine. We must change the narrative about you. Let's show the world the you that I've come to know, and they will love you."

She averted her gaze then, making his heart trip.

Was she implying that she loved him? No, not possible! She couldn't stand the sight of him weeks ago.

No, he was reading too much into her speech.

Moreover, he couldn't forget that she wanted to be the queen, which was the reason she'd married him anyway. So ultimately, she was looking out for herself by wanting him to be king.

He nodded, lowering his gaze so she wouldn't see his dismay at the thought. In any case, if she wanted him to be king, then he would accept her words. Aside from his mother, no one else had told him to his face that he was good enough for the position.

"Okay, let's do it," he said.

"Yeah?" She looked at him, expectantly.

"Yes."

"Great. This is going to be wonderful."

She kissed him, and he scooped her up, heading to the bedroom.

An hour later, while Amara slept, Zik shut the bedroom door and returned to the living room. His mind would not settle while he lay in bed, too concerned for his wife and the current situation in Nigeria. He sat in the armchair and fired off some messages.

First to Razi, his friend in the Bagumi Intelligence Service:

What's the latest on security threats around the Nigerian protestors? I need a briefing ASAP.

Then a message to Lucas:

Send me a list of scheduled dates for the protests at the Nigerian consulate.

Then finally, he called Isha, who was the legal expert. When she answered the phone, he didn't waste time on preambles.

"Sorry to disturb you this late. But I need to pick your brain. What is the legal status on Bagumian royals participating in protests?"

CHAPTER EIGHTEEN

Amara sat in the large conference room listening to Queen Zulekha give a speech about women's role in Bagumian society and maintaining family values to an audience of prominent women in the country.

Also present were Queen Sapphire and Riona. The other princes' wives were not available for the event.

Amara wished she'd had a prior engagement and could've missed this. She tried not to roll her eyes through most of the lecture because it sounded like something suited to her grandmother's era. To distract herself, she sent Zik a message.

Ikemba, kedu?

She didn't get a response back immediately like he normally did. She assumed he was in an important meeting and would reply when he was free. So she switched to social media and checked Zik's page. He'd tweeted, about an hour ago.

Join me and take a stand against police brutality and xenophobia. 2pm. Obiong Square. #weareone #endsars

Amara checked her watch. It showed 14:15 on the digital readout. She checked the posts again. It had been retweeted over ten thousand times. On instinct, she checked his FB page, and he had a live video running.

Her heart stopped, her mouth dropping open.

Zik was at the front of the protest march with thousands of people walking towards Obiong Square, carrying different banners from 'end police brutality' to 'end xenophobia.' All the people wore face coverings over their noses and mouths. Police officers stood at the edges of the crowds. When they reached the square, Zik climbed onto a podium and made a speech.

The video was muted. She couldn't listen because it would have been rude to plug in earphones while at an event. However, she tried to catch some of the automatic speech-to-text transcription.

My wife Amara is a Nigerian. While Nigerians are harassed and brutalised daily by the police who are supposed to protect them, I cannot keep quiet. In the same vein, I cannot be silent when Nigerians living in Bagumi are targeted with acts of hatred. Nigerians are our neighbours, our friends, our brothers and sisters. And like any thriving community, we should protect our neighbours and friends and families.

"What's going on?"

Riona, who was sitting beside her, made her raise her head.

Amara glanced around and shoved her phone in the woman's direction. "It's Zik."

"Wow. This is amazing," Riona replied, watching the video.

"It is. He did it for me. But I didn't know he was going to do this." She was floored, to say the least.

Zik was always supportive. He'd shared her ENDSARS posts and had comforted her when she'd been stressed out about her social media accounts being closed.

However, she hadn't expected him to take it this far and actually go to a rally and address the people. Was this even safe for him? There were police present, and the crowd seemed peaceful.

Still, how would the palace receive his actions? Had they been notified beforehand?

She doubted it, since Zik hadn't even told her. She assumed it was so she could claim plausible deniability. If she didn't know, she couldn't lie about not knowing.

Her hands trembled. Queen Zulekha would have an aneurism when she saw this. It would be yet another reason the woman would dislike Amara, like she seemed to do these days.

Hopefully, the international impact would be positive, and Zik's stock as a serious contender to the throne would be raised although there might be diplomatic issues with Nigeria.

Riona nudged her. "There may be trouble ahead."

On the stage, Queen Zulekha had finished her speech and stepped aside. Her aide approached and whispered in her ear, showing her a phone. Probably the same live stream Amara had watched. The queen's face clouded over, and she glanced in Amara's direction.

"Yep," Amara said. Trouble was coming her way.

"Zik must love you so much to risk her wrath," Riona commented.

Her heart slammed into her chest.

Did Zik love her? Was that why he'd done this?

They had a great relationship, no doubt. After the initial hiccup and makeup, they'd settled into each other. Zik was caring and attentive, a great lover and husband.

The ease with which he opened and expressed himself made her gradually learn to become emotionally naked in front of him. He was always there for her, keeping her safe.

But could a man who had loved so many women, truly love just one? Could she trust that he would never look elsewhere? Her biggest nightmare was waking up one day to an online photograph of her husband in another woman's arms.

"Are you okay?" Riona asked.

She must have seen a frown of Amara's face.

"Yes, I'm fine. I was miles away. I'm worried about Zik. He could get into serious trouble for doing this. He might get demoted or lose his royal status."

"Nah. It won't get that far. He'll get an earful from her, but that's it."

"No." She lowered her voice so no one would overhear. She didn't know why she felt more comfortable with Riona than with the other female spouses. Maybe because they were non-Bagumians. "She doesn't want him to be the future king."

"You can't be serious!"

"I am. She doesn't think he's good enough."

"Who cares what she thinks?"

"You can say that again."

They giggled like co-conspirators, and Amara felt a sense of camaraderie with Riona, which reminded of her relationship with Isha.

She would have to call her best friend as soon as possible and discuss the legal implications of Zik's actions.

Her nape prickled. She looked up and found the first queen glaring at her from across the room.

Uh-oh. She'd managed a small victory by following Queen Sapphire's advice about how to keep the social media accounts open. Her #keepiton tweet had gone viral, and media houses across the world had picked it up, and she'd even done a few online interviews. Queen Zulekha had had to relent and let her keep the accounts because the brouhaha hadn't been good for Bagumi's image internationally.

She wasn't sure Zik's stunt would be so easily pardoned.

***

Three days later, Amara sat in her office going over plans for a 'women in STEM' programme she was setting up. Zik was away on an official trip to Wanai as part of showing support for the new Wanaian government.

Her phone beeped, and she reached for it, hoping it would be a message from Zik taking a break from his itinerary. Instead, it was from Lucas who was away with him.

Mrs Zik, just a heads up in case you don't know yet. Parliament is hearing a bill tomorrow to exclude Zik from the succession.

What on Earth...?

She straightened and pulled her phone from the table. "Salima, please excuse me."

"Your Highness." The woman packed up and left.

She waited until the assistant had shut the door before she dialled Lucas's number. She didn't want to make the call in from of the person she saw as Queen Zulekha's spy.

The phone rang twice before it was picked up.

"Good afternoon, Your Highness," Lucas said.

"Afternoon, Lucas. What's going on? Is my husband okay?"

"Yes, he's fine. He's in an informal meeting with trade ministers at the moment."

"Okay. So, what's this about parliament voting to exclude him?" She was aware that parliament was going to discuss the succession sometime in the future. But Zik was supposed to be present to defend himself, or at least have a spokesperson. The exclusion bill was a new thing.

"A member of parliament has brought forward a bill stating that Zik is unfit to become king because of his recent actions at the protests. There will be a reading of the bill tomorrow."

"What the hell?" Her fury rose.

Ever since the protests had started, people with extremist views had been popping out of the woodwork.

"Who is the MP?" she asked.

"Hissene Ruga."

"Ruga? Isn't Zawadi's fiancée a Ruga?"

"I believe Hissene is Danai's uncle."

What was going on here? Amara was not big on conspiracy theories. But this was beginning to look like one. This could be about getting Zawadi back as the future king. Didn't Zik indicate that Queen Zulekha would rather have Zawadi as the crown prince, come what may? If Zik was disqualified, there was no reason it couldn't revert back to Zawadi if he wanted it. Was the queen responsible for the escalation in anti-Nigerian sentiment?

Amara had to do something. Zik was too far away.

"What time is the bill reading?" she asked.

"I think four p.m.," Lucas replied. "What do you want to do?"

Zik wasn't scheduled to return until afterwards.

"I don't know. Let me think about it. Keep your phone on in case I need to reach you." She ended the call.

She could wait and speak to Zik tonight, but it might be too late to act. So she told Salima she was going for a walk and went in search of Zik's mother.

The queen's advice was to use any means necessary but to keep it legal.

So Amara dismissed Salima for the day, sat down and wrote the script, then set up her recording equipment. Next, she changed her outfit and appearance, before sitting down to deliver an impassioned statement about why her husband should be the future king of Bagumi.

She was halfway through the live stream when the security team burst into the apartment and proceeded to confiscate her recording equipment and digital devices.

Queen Zulekha walked in and told the men to wait outside.

"What is going on here? Amara asked, furious.

"You're under house arrest. You are not allowed to leave these quarters or talk to anyone until further notice."

This was ridiculous. "Why? I haven't committed any crimes."

"You think asking people to protest outside the parliament building tomorrow was clever. But it's an act of treason to incite violence."

"I never incited violence. Peaceful protest is not violence."

"There is a ban on protesting, and you are not above the law."

Had the woman actually hissed those words like a spiteful snake?

Amara shook her head and slumped into the chair. "Why do you hate me so much? What did I do to you?"

"Child, this is not about you."

She raised her head. "This is about Zik, isn't it? You really don't want him to become king."

"He doesn't deserve to become king. He's done nothing but spend his life chasing women. He is the weakest link."

Those words hurt. "That's not true. Zik is a good man. He is the best of the lot."

"No, Zawadi is the best of the lot. My first fruit. He should be king." If the queen had tapped her chest in egotistical pride after that statement, it wouldn't have been surprising.

The tone and sense of misplaced righteousness threw oil on Amara's already red-hot fury.

"Have you seen Zik with young people? The way he connects with them at their level and doesn't condescend to them? Do you know he spent our honeymoon teaching in a school in Beya? At the end of the week, the students didn't want him to leave. Since we got back to Darusa, he's been working so hard I hardly see him. Give him a chance to show you he can be a great king."

Queen Zulekha laughed. "It really is a shame to see how low you've sunken. Now you're defending him. Do you know he gave you up before?"

Amara's stomach curdled. "What do you mean?"

"Zik had the chance to be with you so many years ago. He was in love with you, but he preferred to be with other women, too. Now you think you're special? Do you not know that no matter how sweet he is, how good he is in bed now, he's still going to sleep with other women—"

"Zulekha, stop! That's enough." Queen Sapphire entered the room looking like a lightning storm. "You've gone too far this time."

She pulled Amara into her arms.

"You are the one who spoils these children and makes them think they can defy us and get away with it. Actions have consequences." The snake seemed to have returned.

"Indeed, they do. You will face the consequences for your actions soon, too."

"Just make sure she doesn't leave this apartment. No one is permitted to enter." Queen Zulekha huffed and walked out.

A strange, anti-climactic silence fell like a deadened whoosh over the room after the first consort's haughty departure.

"Mum, what's going on? Can she do this?" Amara finally asked when she'd regained the use of her vocal cords.

Queen Sapphire sighed. "Unfortunately, yes. She is in charge of the women in the palace. But as your husband, Zik can override the decision."

Tears pricked at her eyes. "But I can't even call him. They took my phone and everything."

Her mother-in-law ran a soft hand over Amara's hair. "I'll call him and let him know what happened when I get back to my quarters. I left in a hurry so didn't take my phone."

Still, Amara felt sickened, Queen Zulekha's words playing over and over in her mind.

"She said that Zik had the chance to be with me many years ago. What did she mean?"

Queen Sapphire shook her head. "She had no right to say that to you. That is for Zik to explain. But you should know that Zik loves you."

"You mean the way he loved me years ago and still went sleeping with other women." The tears gathered and fell. It was all too much. Being under house arrest and then finding out about Zik. She'd always known it would come to this.

If he'd given her up once, he could do it again.

Who said he wouldn't?

"Please call my mother when you get to your phone. The marriage trial period ends tomorrow, and I would like to go home."

CHAPTER NINETEEN

Zik sighed in the back seat of the car on the way to the Wanai presidential residence. Isha had invited him for dinner. This trip had been about finding ways to foster a close relationship between Bagumi and Wanai. So far, the outcomes looked great.

He couldn't say the same thing about his relationship with his country. It seemed that while he worked hard to build a better future for his people, they were working hard to oust him from his leadership role.

To be fair, it wasn't the whole country that was against him. Just a select few and powerful people bent on making sure he never ascended to the throne. They'd written a bill that would pass through parliament and ultimately exclude him from the succession.

When Lucas had brought it to his attention earlier today, for the first time since his suitability for the crown had become an issue, he'd almost exploded, incensed and indignant. How dare they try to do this to him? What was his crime? Disqualifying him because of his sex life was ridiculous. He hadn't done any harm to anyone, and his partners had all been consenting adults.

He pulled his phone out and sent Amara a message. He would call her when he had a private moment. But the exchange of text messages helped him get through the days.

Amara had been the one who'd made him realise he had been selling himself short. He'd spent such a great proportion of his life trying not to outshine his older brother that it had become second nature for him to think less of himself.

But spending the last four weeks with Amara had been amazing. She'd seen through his walls, gotten to know the real him, and she actually liked him. That was the best thing ever, considering the contempt she'd held for him at the start of their marriage.

He smiled thinking about that tumultuous first week together. He hadn't thought he would survive that first week let alone last through the month. But they'd done it, and their relationship had grown.

He cringed when he thought about the ultimatum to send her home if she didn't give their relationship a chance. It had been heavy-handed, but it had worked. They had both worked hard at getting on.

If he could take a gamble, he would say that Amara might be in love with him. The way she'd encouraged him to go for the position of crown prince wasn't just about her being the future queen.

She truly believed in his abilities to rule the kingdom. She thought he would be a great king. An awesome one, like she'd said.

And through the days, she'd focused her energy on cleaning up his image and hiring a team to ensure his public image stayed according. He'd even discarded his @playerzik handle in favour of @ikembaprincezik at her suggestion.

The public reception had been good so far. He'd acquired over five hundred thousand new followers in the last week alone. Of course, most of them were Nigerians happy about his involvement in their protests and also because he'd married a Nigerian. Many Igbos even wanted to offer him a chieftaincy title. Some even hyped him as 'Ikemba.'

"Onyi, you should see this." Lucas extended his phone to the middle console separating them in the back seat.

"What is it?" Zik leaned across to watch the flickering screen, and his heart stopped. Amara was on a live video, streaming on her page. What was she doing? "I want to hear this. Increase the volume."

"Hold on," Lucas disconnected his Bluetooth headphones, and the speaker on the phone blasted.

"...my husband is one of those people who goes out of his way to help other people even to his own detriment. But he never asks for help. So I'm asking for your help on his behalf. If Prince Azikiwe has done anything in your community, anything that has impacted you or the lives of your loved ones positively, come out and show your support for him and bring a friend. Let me remind you of the venue—"

Just then, a thumping sound hijacked the video, and footsteps interrupted Amara as she turned to someone off-camera. "What's going on here?"

The video cut off and went blank.

"What happened?" Zik asked, heart racing.

"I don't know. I think she got disconnected," Lucas said.

"Shit. Let it not be what I think." He swiped through his biometric and called her phone number. It rang twice and got cut off. When he called again, it had been switched off.

No! This was not happening.

"Keep trying my wife's number," he said to Lucas and dialled his mother's contact. It rang several times before being answered. "Mum?"

"Your Highness, this is Nenye, Queen Sapphire's assistant. She is unavailable right now," the voice on the other end said.

"Where is she? I need to speak to her."

"I believe she's gone to your palace quarters. Would you like her to call you when she returns?"

"No. I can't reach my wife, and I need to know what's going on. Go to my apartment and give the phone to my mother immediately."

"I'll do that right away." There were rustling sounds, then muffled conversations and footsteps.

As he waited for his mother's aide to get to his quarters at the palace, the car arrived at the presidential residence and he stepped out of the car.

Isha stood at the entrance. He indicated he was on a call, giving her a side embrace. She ushered him and Lucas inside the house and left him in a reception room alone to continue his call.

A few minutes later, Nenye's voice sounded distant. "I need to speak to Her Grace, Queen Sapphire."

A door squeaked open, and footsteps receded. Then seconds later, "Nenye, is there a problem?"

"Your Grace, you have a phone call from Prince Azikiwe." It sounded like Nenye pulled the phone from her pocket because the sound became clearer.

"Thank you, Nenye."

"You're welcome, Your Grace."

A door thudded shut, and his mother voice was in his ear. "Azikiwe, thank goodness you called."

"I tried calling Amara, but her phone is switched off. Where is she?"

"She's here in your apartment."

"Let me talk to her, please."

"Okay. Hold on." It sounded like she moved into another room. "Amara, Azikiwe is on the phone. He would like to talk to you."

"Mum, I don't want to talk to him."

Amara's voice sounded choked and sniffly like she'd been crying. *What?* A door slammed in the distance.

"I'm sorry. She is upset," his mother said in his ear.

"Why is she upset? What happened?" His stomach wrenched that something had upset Amara and he wasn't there to soothe her.

His mother puffed out a heavy sigh. "Zulekha detained Amara and restricted her access to the palace. She can't leave your apartment."

Detained? That was the equivalent of a police arrest and sitting in jail for royals. "What the hell! I'm sorry for swearing, Mum. But why is my wife detained?"

"Don't worry about the swear words. I've uttered a few in recent times because things are just getting too ridiculous here. I think Amara was recording an online video. I don't know if you saw it."

"Yes, I was just watching it before she was disconnected abruptly."

"Yes, Zulekha had the guards seize all the equipment including her phone. That's why you can't reach her. She says Amara broke the law by asking people to show up outside parliament house tomorrow for the reading of the Zik bill. Right now, no one seems capable of stopping her. Your father hasn't curbed her excesses so far. You're the only one who can."

Zik's pulse pounded in his ears, and he panted through his breathing, making his throat dry. That bloody woman! Never mind that he'd considered her as his second mother all his life. A good parent didn't act like a tyrant and get away with it, especially not when they were hurting innocent people. He squeezed his eyes shut and clenched his free hand, trying to quell the surge of rage.

There was no point venting anger on his mother. She was not at fault here. She'd tried so hard to keep the peace for so long. But this time, nothing was going to stop him because he was going to bring the whole fucking house of cards down.

"Mum, I'm not due back in Darusa until tomorrow evening. Please stay with Amara. I don't want her alone in the apartment, feeling like a prisoner. She doesn't deserve this."

"No, she doesn't. I'll stay with her. But there's something else you should know. Zulekha told Amara that you were in love with her a long time ago and still went with other women. That's why Amara doesn't want to talk to you. She's requested to end the marriage and return home at the end of the trial period. I have to call her mother and let her know."

Shit. Zik clutched his head, rubbing his face. His legs gave way, and he slumped into an armchair. The explosions were coming thick and fast. His life would implode if he didn't get a handle on it and soon. His mind went into a black tunnel with a pinprick of light in the distance.

"Azikiwe!"

Someone was calling his name from a distance.

"Zik, are you okay?"

His sister stood in front of him.

"Just give me a minute." He blinked several times, remembering his mother was still on the line. "Sorry, Mum. I'm here. Do me a favour, please. Keep Amara in the palace until I get there."

"I don't know if I can do that. If her people show up to take her home, we will have to let her go."

"I know. But just try and stall them. I'm going to catch the first available flight out. I love her." He choked out. "I can't lose her again."

"I know you love her. She loves you, too."

His heart stalled. "Did she tell you that?"

"No. But it's not difficult to figure out. Amara would not risk Zulekha's wrath if she didn't love you."

"You're right." He sighed as his doubts about his marriage fizzled away. Amara loved him. It was her love for him that made her fight for him, made her want to improve his image, made her want him as king. "It's the reason I can't lose her, Mum. Just keep her safe. I'll be there soon."

"I will. Bye, son."

"Bye, Mum." The call disconnected.

"Zik, what's going on?" Isha asked, drawing his attention.

He placed his phone on the side table. "Did you see Amara's live video broadcast earlier?"

"No." She settled on a chair opposite him. "What is it about?"

He narrated what had happened from the emergency Zik parliament bill to Amara's detention. And just like that, his sister was ready to go to war for him and Amara. Her husband Zain was of the same mind.

But Isha was a one-woman army. She cancelled her appointments for the next few days, arranged childcare for her children, and booked them on an early flight out of Wanai to Bagumi tomorrow.

That night, she called all their siblings, inviting them for an emergency family meeting at Darusa

Palace, timing it to coincide with the Zik bill reading.

Then Zik sat down in one of her reception rooms, and with Lucas's help, recorded a video to be posted online in the morning which would boost Amara's original invitation to protest outside parliament.

That night, he didn't get much sleep. In the morning after a quick breakfast, he posted the video online. Then he, Lucas, and Isha, along with their team of bodyguards, headed to the airport for the four-hour flight.

They arrived at Darusa airport around two-thirty and were picked up by a car convoy. But when they reached the city, they got snagged in traffic at the bottom of Regents Avenue. His phone beeped, and he checked the message from Lucas who sat in a different car.

Your Highness, they came. Look outside.

Zik wound down the tinted window, and his mouth dropped open, his eyes misting.

A sea of people lined the road from the top of Regents Avenue down to Obiong Square and Parliament. It was still about an hour away from the bill reading. But these people had come from different parts of Bagumi and braved the afternoon heat to be here.

There were young people in school uniforms and school buses, too. It seemed some schools had closed for the day and bused their students here. Lucas had told him last night that Principal Bene had spoken to the headteachers union and they had organised today as a school trip for students to visit parliament and witness how it operated. The parents had to give consent, but that didn't seem like it had been an issue.

They all looked like they'd come for a jubilee rather than a protest. He'd emphasised that this was going to be a peaceful march. And they hadn't disappointed him.

Of course, there would be those with the intentions to turn it into a disaster—the reason he had Razi Hamadou and his intelligence team working on the security along with the police.

As Isha had informed him days ago, the crown prince was within his rights to organise a peaceful public march or celebrations. And that's exactly what he'd done.

Yet, this was only one aspect of his plan. He had to get to Amara who was at the palace still under detention.

He depressed the comms button to speak to the driver and security up front. "I need to get out briefly."

"Yes, Your Highness," the bodyguard said. The car engine stopped.

Zik sent a message to Lucas.

I'm going to stop and chat with them briefly. Find me a megaphone or something to use.

The reply came immediately.

Yes, sir.

The car door opened, and Zik stepped out. As soon as the crowd saw him, a big cheer went up, and they started clapping. He waved and walked towards the square where a podium had been set up as his security team cleared the path for him.

Finally, he reached the stage. Thankfully, someone had already set up the mic. He would have to give Lucas and the rest of his team a gift for setting all this up.

He tapped on the mic and it squeaked, making people groan. He chuckled.

"I have your attention now. I am humbled that so many of you showed up today. Thank you. The rally doesn't officially start for another hour, so make yourself comfortable. Each corner of the square has a food stand, so make sure you get some refreshments. It's all on me. The DJ will keep you entertained. Meanwhile, I need to go to my wife. She is still in the palace. We will come back together and address you later. Once again, thank you so much for answering our call."

He stepped away from the mic as the crowd cheered. He waved and hurried down, back to the car. This time, the road was cleared, and they drove up Regents Avenue into Darusa Palace grounds.

He didn't even respond to greetings as he raced to his apartment, Isha and Lucas behind him. Two security guards stood outside his quarters instead of just one, and none of them were his usual team.

"Welcome home, Your Highness." They bowed deep. One of them opened the entrance.

"Thank you," he muttered, squirting gel onto his palm and massaging as he stepped into the foyer and hurried onto the living room.

His mother, Amara, and her brother sat on sofas. As soon as Amara saw him, she hurried into corridor leading to the bedrooms.

"So glad to see you." His mother exhaled in relief as she embraced him sideways.

Isha came in and pulled his mother aside, leaving him to face Amara's brother. The man was only here for one reason. To take her home. But Zik was not ready to let go.

Ekene bumped his elbow. "Dude, we are not happy. Obi adiro anyi mma. Cha cha."

"Ekene, ama m. I know. And I take the blame. Mu nwa ka odi n'isi. Mana i ma na nwanne gi nwanyi ji obi m aka, ji sie ya ike. You know your sister has my heart in her tight grip."

Ekene pursed his lips and nodded. "I know, which is why I was happy to hand her over to you. But this is fucked up. Unu a makwa na o bu adaeze?"

"Of course," Zik replied with the chant they used to tease Amara when they were younger. "Ofu mkpuru adaeze, The one and only princess."

Ekene smiled, shaking his head slowly.

"Let me speak to your sister, please," Zik pleaded, not because he needed the man's permission to speak to his wife, but so he would have Ekene's backing in case things didn't go as planned with the other matters at stake.

"Go." Ekene nodded towards the hallway.

Zik didn't need another prompting and hurried. When he turned the corner, the door to the master bedroom clicked shut. Had Amara been in the hallway listening to their conversation? If she was curious, then perhaps there was some hope for them.

He knocked on the bedroom door and turned the handle when he got no response.

Amara lay on the bed, her back to him. He closed the door and walked to the side of the bed closest to the door and sat on the mattress.

"Babygirl, I'm sorry about what happened," he started.

"Don't call me that."

"Why?"

"Because you probably use it as a generic name for all your floozies so you don't have to remember their names."

Damn, she was cutting deep.

"There has only ever been one babygirl, and she's right here, right now."

"Yeah. Like I'd believe it." She got off the bed, walking to the window.

"It's true. What do I have to do to prove it?"

"Tell me about before, about when you had the chance to be with me but turned it down to go chase women."

He laughed, but it carried no humour, and he massaged his temple.

She swivelled, eyes blazing. "What's so funny?"

"That you think I could ever turn you down is funny." He nearly choked as his throat clogged up, and he stared at his hands on his lap. "Why do you think there were so many other women? It's because I couldn't walk away from you even when I'd promised to leave you alone for my brother."

"You promised to leave me alone?"

Her voice had a shrill but curious ring to it.

"Yes. Many years ago, my stepmother knew, somehow, that I had a thing for you. She summoned me and told me you were betrothed to Zawadi and would get married to him. It had felt like someone had ripped my heart out. I begged her. Told her I loved you. That I'd give up so many other things to Zawadi. The woman laughed at me. Said what did I know about love? That I was only a kid. That I was handsome enough to have thousands of other women. But you were out of bounds."

Amara stood frozen, seemingly captivated by his words. He couldn't read her expression.

"I tried to keep away. But every time I saw you, it was like an itch under my skin that wouldn't go away. And I tried to drown it out with other women. But they were never enough. Never you. Then once, I said fuck it. I was going to have you and to hell with the rest. Remember the masquerade ball at Atlantic Bar? Remember Ikemba?"

Her eyes widened. "That was you? We almost spent the night together."

He nodded. "That was my one act of rebellion. But I couldn't go through with it because I realised it would be using you to get back at my brother and my stepmother, if I'd had sex with you. What kind of person would I be, having sex with my brother's betrothed?"

"But hang on. At that point, I didn't even know Zawadi and I would become an item. It wasn't until after I left university that my parents mentioned the betrothal."

"*I* knew, though. I guess the high queen was reserving you for her son and trying to keep the competition away."

She tilted her head, scrutinising him. "When you married me, you wanted me? It wasn't just an obligation?"

He scrubbed his palms over his face. "Heaven knows I wanted you so much. But it felt like a gift and a curse because you hated me."

She shook her head, clutching her midriff. "I disliked the you that I was brainwashed to see. I thought about it after Queen Zulekha locked me here yesterday. And I realised that for years, she'd filled my head with negative things about you. So each time I saw a photo of you with another woman, it seemed like a validation of my reasons for disliking you."

Zik nodded, a soft sigh escaping him. "It tracks that she would poison you against me. It was all part of her making sure you never considered me as a love interest if I reneged on the promise to leave you alone."

She returned to the bed and sat on the edge, out of reach. "So, you've been in love with me for over ten years?"

He puffed out a heavy breath. "Yes."

"And yet, you were sleeping with other women. How do I know you're not going to cheat on me?"

Another sigh escaped. Guess the time had come to lay down all his cards.

"I guess you *don't* know. I guess you're going to have to take a leap of faith and trust in my promise not to betray you. But I've never cheated on anyone in my life. And you know I couldn't even bring myself to betray my brother with you. If I was going to do it, it would have been then with you. Not now. Not when I've been gifted my heart's desire."

He paused before taking a deep breath. "I know it all seems a bit much, especially with the way you've been treated. But before you decide to end our marriage and hop on a plane back to Nigeria, just give me one more chance to prove my love to you. Isha organised a family meeting. Sit and listen. If you feel your fears haven't been handled appropriately afterwards, I won't stop you from leaving."

His heart raced as he waited for her answer.

"Okay," she said in a soft voice.

The tightness in his chest eased. He nodded and stood. "Come on."

"Wait," she said, standing.

He turned to face her, shoving hands into his pocket to stop from reaching for her. He was struggling to not touch her. They hadn't had physical contact in two days.

"What you told my brother..." she continued.

He raised a brow so she would specify. He'd suspected she'd been listening earlier.

"About your heart in my hands. It's true, isn't it? I have the power to crush your heart."

"Yes, you do." No need trying to pretend. He was all in. No holding back.

"And you have the power to crush mine. Don't make me regret giving it to you," she said, meeting his gaze.

"Never." He stepped forward, euphoria buzzing through him as he cupped her face. "I love you."

"I love you, too." She stood on the tips of her toes, reached for his shoulders, and kissed him.

"Babygirl," he said when he leaned back and reached into his jacket. "Want to see something beautiful? I was going to give you this tonight to celebrate our one-month anniversary. But now is as good a time."

He withdrew the medium-sized jewellery box and opened it, revealing the diamond and multi-gemstones pendant set on a gold chain.

"For me?" she squealed, eyes sparkling like diamonds. "It's so beautiful. Ikemba, happy anniversary. But I don't have a gift for you."

"Omalicha, are you kidding me? You love me. That is solid gold, more precious than jewelleries. Love me from now until eternity, and all our anniversary gifts are covered."

She laughed gloriously. "Deal."

"Now, come on. There's something else I need to show you." He took her hand, and they left the bedroom.

Only Ekene sat in the living room. He eyed them with a grin. "You've made up."

"Of course we've made up." Amara giggled.

"So why did I come out here today?"

"It's like that, huh? You didn't want to see your sister, abi?"

"Ofu mkpuru adaeze. Of course I want to see you."

They all laughed as they headed out of the apartment to the family meeting.

CHAPTER TWENTY

His parents, siblings, and their spouses were already there when they entered. They settled in the vacant chairs, and Riona, who sat closest to Amara, leaned towards her to whisper in her ear.

"The drama's about to hit the fan," her sister-in-law said softly.

Isha had the floor. She glanced at Zik before continuing. "Zawadi, I'm disappointed that you would let this happen. Zik has always had your back. Is it too much to ask for you to have his?"

"Zik has my full support," Zawadi said, drawing taller in his seat, chin pushed out. "I want to make this abundantly clear that I want no part of Mother's machinations. As far as I'm concerned, the crown is Zik's."

"How can you say that? You were born to be king," Queen Zulekha snapped.

"So were my brothers," he gritted out loud enough for everyone to hear. "Ancient Bagumi laws allow for any of the king's children to challenge for the throne."

"And in the spirit of fair challenge, I was representing your interests," the first queen had the audacity to add in a haughty tone.

"Fair challenge?" Zik couldn't keep quiet any longer. He stood slowly from the chair, releasing Amara's hand. "On what galaxy is what you did considered fair challenge?"

Queen Zulekha opened her mouth, saw the cold fury of Zik's face, and closed it.

"Do you consider telling a ten-year-old boy that he would always be second best because he hadn't been born first to be fair? Or laughing and telling a nineteen-year-old that the girl he loved would be given to his brother? That's fair, right."

He looked around the room, and they all seemed horrified.

"Okay. Maybe that's too far back. How about calling me a whore in front of my mother?"

"I wasn't trying to be nasty. I was just stating the truth." Said in that barely bitten out hiss this time.

This had gone too far.

"I don't think you're quite grasping the point, Mother Dearest. Your latest fair challenge included recruiting Danai's uncle to tender a bill excluding me from the succession and whipping up anti-Nigerian xenophobia."

Gasps erupted around the room.

"Please know that my uncle doesn't have mine or my family's support. I am ashamed of his actions, and I'm sorry for the distress it caused you and Amara," Danai jumped up to say.

If Zik was in a forgiving mood, he would have accepted the words, but not today. Still, he gave her a barely perceptible nod. In her own way, Danai was showing him support.

"That aside, the high queen believed it was fair challenge to lock my wife up in her own home and bar anyone else from contacting her. Amara is threatening to return to her father's house. Do you realise that if she leaves, I will go with her, and my feet will not step into this palace again except for father's funeral?"

Another round of gasps, until a deep voice bellowed.

"Azikiwe, watch what you say!"

Zik huffed and suppressed a chortle. Empty words, as always. His wouldn't be today, though.

"Is that all you have to say on the matter, Father? I mean, does nobody know what I am around here? I'm the fixer. I'm the one you assign to the dirty jobs no one else wants to do. Zawadi wants someone to find his friend, I say I'm on it. Isha wants to send spies into Wanai, I get it done. Mother Dearest wants me to quit the woman I love, I say why don't you gut me but hey, we're all family. Father wants someone to complete the marriage contract with the Onohs, and I step up."

Silence met those words, but that wouldn't deter him. Zik walked toward the dais and stared straight at Queen Zulekha.

"If you didn't want me to be king, you could've just asked me to give it up, and I would have done so. Instead, you threatened my wife. Are you fucking insane?"

"Azikiwe, I won't warn you again!"

Zik snarled this time.

"Father, do you think I came here to make peace?" He laughed coldly.

"Then why are you here?" his father asked in an impatient tone.

He turned and met the old man's gaze. "This is a takeover. Your response determines how hostile it gets."

"Excuse me?"

"You heard me. Have you looked out of the window in the past hour? Someone please show the king one of the live streams from Obiong Square."

Zawadi stepped up and handed his phone to their father.

"What is this?" The king looked up from the screen.

"It's what your wife tried to stop when she arrested my wife. Those people are there to support me. They believe that I can be a good king. They believe in me. Something that seems to be rare in my family."

"Zik—"

"What?"

He swivelled, ready to lay into whoever had dared interrupt him.

His siblings stood, one by one, and came to stand behind him. Zawadi, Kalahari, Zediah, Zareb, Isha, India, and Amira.

"We met before you arrived. You should know you have our support—all of us," Kal spoke.

Zik's eyes narrowed. "All of you?"

"Yes!" they chorused.

He nodded, a little choked up to speak immediately, and then gave a sideways glance. "Thank you."

They patted his shoulders, and he faced their parents. "I have demands, and they are to be met in their entirety."

"Fine. Name them," the king said.

"First, the exclusion bill dies. Tonight."

"W—" Queen Zulekha started, but his father raised his hand, cutting her off.

"Done," the king said.

"Secondly, she goes. Queen Zulekha retires from active duty. She will confine herself to the Lake Miri residence and will only be allowed at Darusa Palace on specific occasions signed off by me."

"No way! Not happening!" Zulekha retorted.

"Do I need to remind you? This is not a negotiation," Zik snapped.

"Azikiwe, why are you doing this?" his father asked in a subdued voice.

"I'm doing this because your wife is a threat to my wife's safety. I can't have her in a position of power over Amara or any other woman in this palace. She caused my wife a lot of distress. If my mother hadn't intervened, it would have been more traumatic. That can never happen again. She can't live here. She should retire and find a new hobby. And while she's there, she can reflect on her treatment of Riona and Danai and the trauma her actions caused Kalahari."

Silence settled as Queen Zulekha tried to sputter away.

"Done," his father pronounced.

"No, Ibrahim. I'm your first wife!"

The king turned fully to her. "And he's my son. You overextended yourself this time. You shouldn't have arrested her."

"But she was inciting protests. I was protecting the country."

King Ibrahim shook his head. "It's not *your* job to protect the country. Sometimes, you act as if you're the king rather than the consort. Azikiwe is right. You need to focus on other things. Take up the art lessons you've always wanted to do. It'll be good for your soul. Maybe you will reflect on your past actions. But you are relieved of royal duties with immediate effect. Sapphire is now in charge of your previous duties and will delegate hers as she sees fit."

The room fell into silence once again because something significant had happened. Zik hadn't actually been expecting his father to give in so readily. He'd expected to get bloody first.

His father looked up at him, and for the first time in years, seemed to gaze at him with respect.

"So, Azikiwe, do you have any other demands?"

Some of Zik's anger ebbed away. "Yes, Dad. I have one more. You challenged me to become a better person worthy of the crown. I know that I am suitable to take on the role when it eventually gets to me. Therefore, I demand that the interim crown prince position be made permanent."

His father started laughing, a full belly heart laughter, making other people break out in smiles as they watched him.

"For a moment, I thought you were going to demand to be made the king right away." His father clutched his chest. "If all you want is the crown prince position, then that's a relief because it's yours. I never intended to give it to anyone else."

The rest of the room erupted into laughter, dissolving the high tension instantly.

Smiling, Zik turned to Amara and extended his hand. She placed hers in his and rose from the chair.

"You heard him. Omalicha, you are the future queen."

A present he was delighted to give her. The most beautiful person on the planet had been presented to his brother on a platter, and he'd turned her down. Now, the gift was his, and he would forever be grateful for her love.

"And you, my Ikemba, are the future king."

Thank you for reading The Future King. If you enjoyed this story, please leave a review at the site of purchase.

Want to read an extended epilogue and find out what happened next with the characters, as well as other book news? Sign up for my newsletter at:

www.kirutaye.com/contact

ROYAL HOUSE OF SAENE

THE PRINCESSES:
His Defiant Princess by Nana Prah

His Inherited Princess by Empi Baryeh

His Captive Princess by Kiru Taye

THE PRINCES:
The Torn Prince by Zee Monodee

The Resolute Prince by Nana Prah

The Tainted Prince by Kiru Taye

The Illegitimate Prince by Empi Baryeh

The Future King by Kiru Taye

Royal House of Saene Spinoffs

Saving Her Guard by Kiru Taye (Latifah and Kojo from His Captive Princess) OUT NOW

Screwdriver by Kiru Taye (Oumou and Yahya from The Tainted Prince) COMING SOON

OTHER BOOKS BY LOVE AFRICA PRESS

Love on a Mission by Jomi Oyel

Note Worthy by Dhasi Mwale

Forever and a Day by O.L. Obonna

Scar's Redemption by Kiru Taye

CONNECT WITH US

Facebook.com/LoveAfricaPress

Twitter.com/LoveAfricaPress

Instagram.com/LoveAfricaPress

www.loveafricapress.com

www.ingramcontent.com/pod-product-compliance
Lightning Source LLC
Chambersburg PA
CBHW020806190726
48285CB00006B/2174